Another Place

Another Place:
Brief Disruptions

Edited by Ashley Cyr

Another Place:
Brief Disruptions

Copyright © 2016 by Ashley Cyr

Cover by: John Ryers

ISBN-13: 978-0-9949210-3-1
ISBN-10: 0-9949210-3-9

Bushmead Publishing
www.bushmead.com

Printed in U.S.A

Acknowledgements:

Special thanks to my parents for believing in me,
to Adam Alldis for designing a beautiful cover,
and to my dog for kindly sparing
my notes on this anthology.

In part supported by

ONTARIO ARTS COUNCIL
CONSEIL DES ARTS DE L'ONTARIO

Contents

Since founding of Bushmead, it has been my desire to curate this collection. I love the idea that even in our deeply flawed – but slowly improving – world, there are artists and dreamers imagining another place, another time, where things are different. Where some situations are better, some worse, and where our conceptions of them are challenged in some way or other.

Issues around sex and gender have been, and continue to be, pressing, not only politically, but also in the imagination of our collective cultural consciousness. News stories about legislation of bodies and prevention of expressions of self and love plague our Twitter feeds, often overshadowing victories, big or small.

What they all come down to is a problem of empathy, understanding, and at the heart of it, imagination. Too often we are unable, or unwilling, to imagine the nuances of identities other than their own. We are unable to understand the need for women to have control over their own reproductive systems; the need for non-traditional families to have the same access to the same benefits; the need for transgender people to be able to express their identities without encountering violence from a system ostensibly built to protect the people.

This is a problem of imagination, and it is there that we may find a solution. What the authors in this collection have created engrossing stories to transport the reader into another place, another identity. Perhaps one of the greatest things that art does for humanity is facilitate empathy. While it is impossible for our legislators and ourselves to physically embody minority identities, we can for a time, with a book in hand, come closer to understanding the implications of these identity politics for individual people both between the pages and on the streets.

Most of the stories and poems you will find between these covers are set in completely unrecognizable climes, while others are located somewhere we may recognize, but through the eyes of another identity. What each one of them has in common is characters grappling with issues at the heart of our North American debates about gender and sexuality.

I, and many other scholars, have found that speculative fiction is a particularly conducive literary locale to have these discussions. It takes the identity politics out of the known venue of policy debates, and places them somewhere else. Perhaps you will find that once those same issues, under represented on the twenty-four-hour news cycle are set in new light, you will come to a new understanding of the issues, and the people they affect every day both here on Earth and in another, imagined place.

- Ashley Cyr, 2016

Will J Fawley is a proposal writer by day and a speculative fiction writer by night. He was developed in the mountains of Virginia and now operates in Winnipeg. He holds an MFA from George Mason University where he was assistant fiction editor for Phoebe Journal of Literature and Art. His short fiction has appeared in The Northern Virginia Review and Sassafras Literary Magazine, and his book reviews have appeared in The Winnipeg Review and As It Ought to Be. When he's not writing about business or spaceships, he can often be found playing video games or herding cats.

http://willjfawley.com/about/

The Gravity Of Desire
by Will J Fawley

The birth count this October hit a record low, dropping nearly 15% from September's total. As such, new D-zire skins will be made available to anyone with an assigned Optimal Reproductive Partner (ORP) who is in possession of a registered D-vice. Remember, failure to meet the daily attempted reproduction quota with your Optimal Reproductive Partner (ORP) will result in a full ban from D-zire Augmented Pleasure for three months. Do your part to save humanity!

"Come on, let's finish," Jezz said when the announcement ended. We had stopped to listen to the system-wide message -- or rather, it stopped us when the chips implanted behind our ears fed it directly into our brains. Jezz was used to ignoring the messages, but for some reason they always pulled me away from whatever I was doing.

I looked over at Jezz beside me, my lawfully wedded ORP, her eyes closed. Of course they weren't her eyes I was seeing, but I knew she was the one I was really touching. "I can't," I said.

"We've still got a couple hours before midnight. We can try again later." Jezz pulled her gown loose from the tangled sheets and slid into it. "Can you imagine," she said as the fabric slid over her head, "being banned from D-zire? It must be awful."

"Maybe it's not so bad?"

"Not so bad? It's primitive, attempting reproduction with someone you're not attracted to."

"I don't know, maybe if you're attracted to your ORP..."

"Are you attracted to me?"

"No."

"Good. Me neither."

Smog curled against the window like it was trying to get

in.

"Do you ever think maybe it's not just about the reproduction?" I asked.

"Well, of course it's not just about the act of attempted reproduction. It's about the children. Isn't that what you mean, Dack?"

"I don't know."

"Jesus, Dack!" Jezz smacked her pillow in frustration, and then pulled it to her chest. "I'm trying to be patient with you and your soul-searching, I really am. But you're not the only one who's going to be in trouble if we don't meet our quota." She put the pillow down and chewed at a scab on her lip. "Maybe something's wrong with your D-zire -- it's not syncing right or something."

"I keep trying to tell you, D-vices are self-repairing and all their software updates automatically. There's never anything wrong with D-zire."

"I'm only trying to help," she said. "I just don't understand why D-zire isn't enough for you anymore. Do you?"

"That's what I'm trying to figure out." I held her hand in mine and our eyes met. There was something desperate there in her face, searching. But it faded as she sat back against her pillow and loaded something on her D-vice.

As I watched her stare blankly ahead, I found myself wishing that D-zire could be enough, as it had been in the honeymoon period when Jezz and I actually enjoyed each other's company.

I sat back beside Jezz and loaded up my newsfeeds. As I scanned through the words I'd see a link that interested me and then scroll past it looking for something better until it all became an endless string of information. I wasn't going to get any reading done.

"Who do you make love to?" I asked.

"What the hell does that mean, Dack?"

"It's something I read in a micro once. It's what they used to call attempted reproduction before D-zire."

"Jesus, Dack. You always bring up these stupid ideas --

things you read, things you're unhappy about. If you didn't spend so much time thinking about things that make you miserable, you might actually be happy for once."

"Sorry." I put my hand on her arm. "But you didn't answer my question."

She let out a long, slow breath. "You're not going to let this go, are you?"

I shook my head.

"Here in the real world?" she said. "I'm loving you."

"No, I meant who do you D-zire?"

"Isn't that a little personal?" Jezz massaged the back of her neck. "Go in for chip maintenance, Dack. Maybe get them to reinstall your D-zire so we don't have this problem again. I know it's not your fault, but even when I'm with a skin, I can still feel you, feel that you're not into it. And no offense, but I don't want them to shut off my D-zire."

Be ready for your partner. Download new skins today. Blink twice to select a package and have what you most D-zire.

When the announcement ended, I looked up and down to scroll through a few packages of skins suggested based on my recent body scans. The guys I scanned on a day-to-day basis didn't really have anything in common -- I didn't really care who they were as long as they weren't Jezz -- so the suggested skins were of all body shapes and sizes and wore everything from priest's robes to studded leather harnesses. I felt a small victory in stumping D-zire's ability to categorize my preferences.

Jezz lay right next me, but our limbs were carefully arranged in a way that allowed us no contact. She seemed so far away. Impossible to touch. Further than any D-zire experience.

"Dack?"

"What?"

"Go get your chip fixed."

"Fine, I will."

"Really?"

"Yes, really."

"Okay, now let's go again before they shut off our D-zire."
I selected a package at random. The program loaded and
a tingle spread through my head as the augmented reality
interface fed in from the D-vice chip behind my ear, sending
the data through to my ocular nerves. As the skin loaded,
Jezz's body transformed into one I was actually attracted to.

Since D-vices were self-repairing, there was only one
physical tech support clinic, which was mostly for show. It
was located on the 5 square-mile D-vine campus that had
been built over several historic downtown neighbourhoods.

The tech support clinic was on the fifty-first floor of the
headquarters building, the prestigious One D-vine Drive. The
building itself was a blue glass skyscraper fashioned after the
Burj Dubai, which it surpassed in height by three-point-two
inches.

The lobby was a cavernous room. The ceiling must have
been a good fifty floors up, but the distance was hard to judge
through the flock of artificial clouds above. I took a glass
elevator up through the clouds, and when I got to the tech
support clinic, an infert at the front desk asked me to fill out
a novel-length form and upload it to the D-vine file system,
'clouDnine'.

I'd never really looked at an infert before, you know,
really looked. Infert men were not allowed to wear any sort of
facial hair, and their smooth cheeks often gave them a child-
like appearance. But this man's face wasn't child-like at all.
His jaw was strong, and I admired the contour of his cheeks,
his sculpted chin and exposed lips. I tugged at my own beard,
which suddenly felt like a mask.

I must have been staring at the infert, because he said, "Sir,
you can wait right over there," and motioned to a sitting area
where a bald guy sat across from a woman with two children
who chased each other around the empty chairs. Chips never
malfunctioned. Baldy was probably a hypochondriac, and the

woman just a concerned mother. All of our chips were fine. I was sure of it. And yet here I was.

I took a seat a safe distance of five chairs away from baldy and scanned through some newsfeeds, the words projecting themselves directly into my eyes so it looked like they were inlaid across the room before me. I quickly found myself absorbed by a micro about a bizarre concept from the early 21st century. It was called overpopulation. People had once been concerned about the possibility of overcrowding the planet. I shook my head and laughed to myself. They had spent all their time worrying about this possibility and had never considered the alternative. I was so busy reflecting on the short-sightedness of my ancestors that I didn't realize baldy and mother had already been called back. The tech will see you in room 2, scrolled across the micro.

"So you've been having problems with your D-zire?" the tech asked as he scratched at his beard.

"Yes."

"What kind of problems?"

"I don't know if they're problems exactly. But something just hasn't felt right lately."

"Any pain or swelling around your chip? Headaches?"

"No, nothing like that."

"Hold still and close your eyes." I did as I was told and my eyelids went red as the scanner spun 360 degrees around me and read my chip.

"It seems to be working fine, but I do see you had a bit of trouble during attempted reproduction last night."

I looked at the tech's nametag -- Suresh -- then down at my boots.

"These things happen."

"They do?"

"Sure. Attraction is only partly visual. The first D-zires were rejected by half of the early adopters, until we came up with an override for the less tangible aspects of attraction."

"And what are those less tangible aspects?"

"Look at you, trying to get me to give up confidential

D-vine information. Do you want me to lose my job?"

"No, of course not, I was only…"

"I'm just teasing you. Relax, you'll be fine. You'll get back in the game. Just don't take too long or we'll have to ban you from D-zire. That won't be necessary though, will it?"

I shook my head.

"Good. Like I said, don't worry. I can give you an override for the unsuccessful reproduction attempt notifications. Just for a couple weeks, until I have a chance to monitor your performance and verify that you're back on track."

"You mean, you can see? You watch when…"

"Of course. Well, not me personally, not all the time. But how else would we know your D-zire is working?"

Suresh chuckled and when he turned his head to look at me, his beard covered his name-tag. For some reason I thought of the infert in the lobby and how vulnerable and exposed he was. How open.

"So there's nothing wrong with my D-zire or my chip then?"

"Nope. Your D-zire has installed all of its automated updates and seems to be working fine. And chips are…"

"Self-repairing, I know. My ORP made me come."

Suresh nodded and smirked as if he had heard this excuse many times. "Good luck. You know, D-vine has made several new skins available, you might download a new package and find something to make things run a little smoother." He actually winked.

"Thanks."

As I walked back through the lobby, the infert was talking to the woman from before. I don't know what I was thinking, but while they were both distracted by the kids, I touched the chip behind my right ear and scanned his beardless face and infert body into my D-zire.

I have to admit, I had kind of hoped there was something

wrong with my D-zire, something I could've blamed that unwarranted sense of dissatisfaction on. But as I climbed into bed with Jezz that night and loaded the infert's skin over her body, I had to accept the fact that my D-zire was working just fine.

And yet, still something nagged at me, a longing for something even more abstract than D-zire. The harder I tried to isolate the feeling, the further it slipped away from me. I couldn't say what it was--I couldn't even describe the feeling other than to say the absence of whatever I longed for tugged at me like the intangible gravity of dark matter. I opened my eyes and my D-zire commanded the skin of the infert to open his eyes too, their irises brown and warm. His pupils grew wide as they took me in, beckoning me to fall inside. And yet I knew Jezz's green eyes were somewhere on the other side of the skin. Were they open or closed?

The infert whispered in my ear, and I wondered if his deep voice muffled Jezz's moans. As I reached down and touched the infert's body, I knew his warmth was hers. No matter how far apart our D-zires were, our bodies were locked together in the most intimate way.

My mind tugged me out of the moment again and I pulled away from the infert/Jezz. I was planning to take a quick break and try again, but as I turned off my D-zire and Jezz came back into focus, I realized I had an excuse.

"I think my D-zire is broken again," I said.

Jezz put a finger against my lips and pulled me back toward her. "Quiet, Strauss. Keep going!"

"Strauss, as in Strauss your boss?" I asked. "Is your D-zire still on?"

"Oh, yes. Sorry." She turned it off. I think.

I rolled over so I didn't have to look at her.

"Dack?"

"Yes?" I said without turning around.

As Jezz slid her nightgown over her head, she spoke through the fabric, "The tech told you they would turn off my reporting too, right?" And as her head emerged, "I won't lose my D-zire if we don't..."

"You and Strauss will live happily ever after."

"Okay. Goodnight then." She blinked three times, signalling her optical sensor to turn the lights off.

"Night."

I looked through the darkness, trying to pinpoint the exact corner where the two walls met the ceiling. There was that dark matter tug again. Why had I done it, scanned the man at the support clinic? Surely I wasn't attracted to an infert, an undesirable. The room suddenly felt too hot and a bead of sweat dripped from my hairline. There had to be a law against it -- D-vine must have received an alert the moment I scanned him. But no, I remembered, there were no rules against who you could and couldn't scan. That was the beauty of it. You were free to D-zire anyone, because it wasn't real. It did no harm and there was no judgment as long as you did your duty with your Optimal Reproductive Partner. Then why did I feel such shame?

I blinked, and in the darkness that overtook the room I couldn't tell if my eyes were open or closed.

The next morning I woke to find that Jezz had already left for work. The room was cold without her, and I wondered how I could both want and not want her at the same time.

Our chips were linked by holy matrimony, allowing Jezz and I to track each other's movements at any time. Even though there was nothing wrong with my D-zire, I'd told her I would get my chip looked at again. I had to go through the motions of visiting the D-vine campus so she'd see that I went there.

When I reached the campus, I pulled up my coordinates. If Jezz checked on me, she would see that I'd gone to the edge of campus, but no further. She wouldn't check. She wouldn't care. She'd be too busy looking for the next Strauss to scan -- her assistant, or if her attraction was all about power, maybe

Strauss's boss.

The dark matter feeling tugged me in all directions. I wanted to see the infert again, but I didn't. I wanted and didn't want him much like I wanted and didn't want Jezz. The pull of curiosity won though, and I justified it by telling myself I'd better go into the tech lab on the off chance that Jezz checked my coordinates.

My heart dropped when I saw the blonde woman at the front desk. She clicked her glowing synth-nails against the projection keyboard and glanced between two screens. I turned around, resigned to go back to Jezz and find a way to complete another attempted reproduction. We'd done it thousands of times. Surely I could force myself to forget that there was a person on the other side of the skin. Just one more time. And another after that. Until we achieved successful reproduction or we died, whichever came first. Hopefully death, because the baby option would only get me off the hook for a six month rest. Then it would be back to fighting off the horrible feeling that there was another barrier between us besides the skins.

As I was about to exit the tech clinic, the infert entered through the automated glass doors. He smiled when he saw me and I noticed that his pupils were as big and black as their counterparts in my D-zire -- and they had just as much gravity.

"Hi," I said.

"Hi." He slowed as he approached me, as if he wanted to say something. But we didn't speak and he kept walking to the desk.

I took a seat in the waiting area and watched across the room as the blonde woman said something to him that I couldn't hear. Then she stepped out from behind the desk and a smile twisted up the corner of her mouth for a moment as she walked by me and out the door.

I looked around the empty waiting room and then walked up to the front desk.

"Do you have an appointment?" the infert asked.

"No..."

"What was your name again?"

"Dack," I said.

"Nice to meet you, Mr. Dack. My name is Stayen and I will be assisting you. Again."

"It's just Dack, actually. Nice to meet you too." I stuck out my hand and when he wrapped his fingers around mine I felt a warm sensation ripple through my abdomen. I'd never touched someone I'd been attracted to before. I'd only glimpsed illusions of attraction as I touched my ORP. "You're uh...you have a nice jaw."

"Thank you, Mr. Dack."

"Just Dack."

"Yes, I'm sorry, Mr. Dack." He didn't look sorry.

"No, I'm sorry. That was rude of me. It's just... I don't see many inferts and, oh god there I go again..."

"It's okay, Mr. Dack. They keep us pretty well-hidden, ensuring that upstanding citizens such as yourself never have to face the inconvenience of running into an undesirable outside the D-vine campus."

I forced a laugh, hoping he was joking, and then looked down at the ground.

"So what brings you here today? Is your D-zire still 'malfunctioning?'"

"Yes. I mean no, it's fine."

"So how can I help you?"

"I don't know."

"There must be some reason you're here."

"I don't know. There isn't. I mean, yeah there is, but..."

"Let me guess, you've come to mock the poor infert and his hairless face. Why are you breeders so fascinated by us?"

"No, it's not that. Well, I mean you are interesting and all, but..."

"I am?"

"Yes. I mean no. I don't know."

The infert laughed. I lifted my head, my eyes grazing up the stainless steel desk, up Stayen's periwinkle vest, his wide neck and jaw, and finally pulled in by the gravity of his gaze. My tension snapped and came out as a broken laugh.

"I'm sorry for before," Stayen said. "It's just that I get that a lot. Assholes coming in to laugh at me and the other inferts. They're 95% of the visitors we get. Makes me defensive. But you're obviously not the type. If you're not here to laugh at me, what do you want, Dack? There must be something I can help you with. New skins for your D-zire?"

"I already have a good one," I muttered, unsure if I wanted him to hear me or not.

"What?"

"Nothing. You wouldn't understand."

"I wouldn't?" he challenged.

"No, you can't use D-zire."

"I can't?"

A bead of sweat dribbled down my nose in warning, but I opened my big mouth anyway. "No, you're an infert. You can't. Can you?"

"Of course inferts can use D-zire! But when you're not bound by the reproduction laws, you don't really need it."

"But you don't have an Optimal Reproductive Partner. I mean, you can't..."

"No, we can't make babies."

"So how do you..."

"A child isn't the only thing two people can make."

That night as I was lying next to Jezz, I knew something had to change. Whatever force was tugging at me would surely pull me apart. I couldn't go on like this. But at the same time, my life with Jezz was all I knew. Maybe we could change together? "I want to try it without D-zire tonight," I said.

"I thought you got your chip fixed. You went to the D-vine campus."

"I did go there. But there was never anything wrong with my chip."

"I don't understand. Then what's wrong?"

"Can we just try it?"

"Are you crazy? You can't even perform as it is. How is the lack of D-zire going to help anything?"

"I don't know."

"We're not attracted to each other, Dack. We won't reproduce."

"Maybe we will. We won't know unless we try."

"Then we'll never know."

"Just one time. And if it's awful we turn on our D-zires and pretend it never happened."

"You don't get it, Dack."

"Get what?"

"It's not about us. It's about the future, the children."

"What children?"

"Exactly."

I looked at her -- at her -- not some skin over her. And I saw that she was as scared as I was. "Is it worth it?" I asked. "Bringing children into a world where people push each other further away the closer they get?"

"Of course it's worth it. This is the only world we have. It's the only way we can save our species from extinction."

"But what kind of life is this -- for us, for them?"

"I don't know. But it's a life. And that's enough. It has to be." Jezz started crying and I pulled her into my arms. She didn't resist, but still she felt so far away, even as her wet face pressed against my chest. I kissed her tears, and then dried her face with the sheets and kissed her mouth. It was the first time in our 14 year assignment that my lips had touched hers without D-zire.

Stayen flashed through my mind, his own lips full, strong, and inviting without a mustache to hide them.

Jezz was right, she had been right all along. It was never about us.

I kissed her again. "I'm sorry. But I have to leave."

"Where are you going, Dack?" she asked as I pulled on my clothes. "When are you coming back?"

"I don't know," I said as I opened the door.

Fiction writer, poet, and playwright J. J. Steinfeld lives on Prince Edward Island, where he is patiently waiting for Godot's arrival and a phone call from Kafka. While waiting, he has published sixteen books, including Our Hero in the Cradle of Confederation (Novel, Pottersfield Press), Should the Word Hell Be Capitalized? (Stories, Gaspereau Press), Anton Chekhov Was Never in Charlottetown (Stories, Gaspereau Press), Would You Hide Me? (Stories, Gaspereau Press), Misshapenness (Poetry, Ekstasis Editions), Identity Dreams and Memory Sounds (Poetry, Ekstasis Editions), and Madhouses in Heaven, Castles in Hell (Stories, Ekstasis Editions). His short stories and poems have appeared in numerous anthologies and periodicals internationally, and over forty of his one-act plays and a handful of full-length plays have been performed in Canada and the United States.

http://www.ekstasiseditions.com/recenthtml/madhouses.htm

http://www.ekstasiseditions.com/recenthtml/identitydreams.htm

Worldly Musings on Otherworldy Love and Desire
By J. J. Steinfeld

The Beginning of an Intergalactic Love Affair

The recently divorced man of average height, early fifties, and above-average longing, a man who had always considered himself unlucky at love and sexually maladroit despite his strong passions, during one of his usual late-night walks along the city's waterfront boardwalk met a newly arrived space alien. She was tall, ageless, and eerily lovely. The late-night walks were part of the man's unalterable routine and seemed to enable him to deal with what he regarded as a monotonous life, romantic setbacks and frustrations, and a tedious, soul-numbing job with the same municipal government department for three decades. But his monotonous life, the ordinariness of his everyday existence, he realized without much deliberation, was now irrevocably altered.

At first the man was frightened, as if meeting a snarling ghost or mythic monstrous creature yet it was only an otherworldly visitor with a refined accent and an impressive vocabulary. Obviously, the man thought, the space alien had somehow studied Earth languages and what he was hearing seemed to be a strange amalgam of several languages but with enough English that he could understand what was being said to him. The man had loved science-fiction films and stories since he had first learned to read, so it wasn't as if he hadn't done his research, in a peculiar manner of speaking. But in none of the hundreds of stories and films had he come across anything so astonishing and appealing. (Yes, appealing was how he was regarding the space alien, though at first he was uneasy with this difficult to describe attraction.) In fact, two nights ago, after returning from his late-night walk, he had stayed up all night and re-watched on DVD some of his favourite old science-fiction films, starting with the original 1953 War of the Worlds and finally falling asleep at five-thirty in the morning during the climatic last scene of 1977's Close Encounters of the Third Kind, a film he had watched more times than he could count but didn't contain anything that remotely resembled the space alien he was now near enough to touch.

As he continued to look at the space alien's beautifully oblong, glistening, variegated, and oddly-textured face that he was eager to caress, the man imagined himself and the space alien in his living room, sitting on his worn couch together and watching some of his large collection of science-fiction films that he cherished, especially a few of the classics first shown before he was born. Suddenly, he realized, he had no idea what age this space alien might be, but concluded age was the least of the perplexing questions that would need answering sooner or later, and certainly shouldn't be an impediment to what he hoped would be open and honest communication between two dissimilar yet receptive life forms.

After a silence of wondrous dread and dreadful wonder, he cleared his throat and stammered forth, Pleased to meet you, my dear, not knowing if what he was addressing was female, male, or something outside of gender and category.

More silence, inspection of their respective otherness up and down, down and up, he wide-eyed and baffled, the space alien glowing-eyed and knowing. He estimated the space alien was around seven feet tall, but well proportioned, and dressed in some sort of loose-fitting space suit that didn't detract from the space alien's attractiveness. He tried to imagine the space alien without the space suit and caught himself imagining the body of his ideal woman. That, he knew, was ludicrous to contemplate. If he was ever fortunate to see the space alien without any space-travel accoutrements, he was certain it would be like nothing he had ever seen before, and that excited him even more. Imagination, he knew, was an aphrodisiac of great potency.

Time passed, earthly time, neither of the two moving far from each other, a little get-to-know-you conversation, some reassuring small talk, an interlude of suggestive erotic storytelling followed by philosophical discourse, the far-travelling interlocutor answering the this-world-man's questions with polysyllabic words half of which he didn't know. Yet he was amazed what could be communicated with facial expressions and gestures.

Finally, the pretentious space alien dropped all pretence and made a sound it would take the recently divorced man ten lifetimes to describe, then he was kissed on the lips, tongue and tongue-like meeting in transcendent ecstasy, taking him to other planets, knowing in his earthbound heart of hearts love was right around the intergalactic corner.

The Sexual Desire of a Space Creature

The space creature, an outcast from his own planet who had lived successfully and undetected among the inhabitants of Earth for two decades, had waited all those long Earth years to make an attempt to communicate sexually with an Earthling. For the entire time, the sexual ways of the inhabitants of Earth had baffled yet intrigued him, and he had spent innumerable hours in front of a computer screen studying their fascinatingly odd sexual behaviour, even learning to pleasure himself in ways that were unheard of on his planet.

When he found the tallest, strongest, most sturdy woman possible standing in front of the boarded-up old tavern near his apartment building, he dissolved his Earthling disguise and showed her his actual visage, which had no adequate Earth words for description. On his planet, the space creature would be called sqixellix, which roughly translates as "virile." He offered the woman immortality as the first Earthling to fornicate with a visitor from another planet, and she said, "A hundred bucks, buddy." The space creature looked in his wallet and there was nothing. The perfect woman for interplanetary fornication walked away.

On Meeting a Goth Androgyne in a Dark Downtown Bar

The brooding darkly dressed
goth androgyne (I doubt if I can
give a better description)
stands next to me at the bar
expensive drink in hand
and tells me unprompted,
"It's dark and getting darker,"
and I smile, bewildered into curiosity,
offering to buy the dark-worshipping
goth androgyne another drink
less expensive, though,
darkly accepted, then,
a long-fingered hand
waved pointing at the occupants
of the bar, "Look at their ersatz agony
and meaningless posturing."
Thoughts of identity and authenticity
upending my psyche and sadness
I detect the scent of schadenfreude
we share yet another cathartic libation
(the goth androgyne's mischievous phrase)
altogether three drinks worth of dialogue
about sex on Earth and sex
on other misdefined planets
and I ask, What sex or gender
do you prefer, in morning or nighttime?
And what is gender on other planets
and if it's bright will you miss the darkness?
A subtle laugh, a refreshing smile
teeth marvellously gleaming
I estimate I'm twice the age
and three times the angst
of the amiable goth androgyne

but who's counting or deconstructing.
I say, my farewell assertion,
At least you know exactly who you are,
a feeble insight catching me by the throat,
relinquishing bewilderment like an exhausted night
grudgingly relinquishes darkness.

A Godly Magic Trick

She came up to me in the lobby of the movie theatre, I about to find a seat for the remake of a science-fiction film I had first seen as a little boy with my father, and now looked forward to seeing alone fifty-seven years later, and she told me I looked remarkably like her husband, who had died of a drug overdose two years ago. In fact, she said, it will be exactly two years in two days. I didn't know what to say to the attractive woman, perhaps half my age, and who looked remarkably like my mother, at least how I remember my mother when I was a young man, but I didn't want to mention that. My mother had died over forty years ago, but I couldn't recall the date, only that it was during winter and I was still a teenager.

"I'm as fearful as the sea," the woman says in a stuttering orator's voice. Yes, this woman reminds me of my youth before a disorderly life became an orderly, middle-class existence.

"I'm as confused as the sand," I say to the woman, not sure if I am being serious or attempting to undermine what she is saying, to attempt to impress the woman with my wittiness or to push her away with my disrespect, and I refuse to return to my youth before or after the orderliness.

"Does God become bored? Does God sometimes ask the wrong questions? Does God wish for the night to end?" the woman asks, her stuttering becoming more pronounced.

As I begin to answer, prepared to speculate or offer gentle lies to all her questions, she disappears in the middle, I assume, of a godly magic trick.

An Unhappily Married Couple Watch an Old Sci-Fi Film on Late-Night TV

Hester and Artie watched as, on screen, a voracious female space alien unceremoniously devoured a luckless male Earthling. Hester asked her husband if he thought the scene was a metaphor for the mating habits of praying mantises. He told her not to be stupid and pulled down his pants, claiming the scene had excited him. Hester finally told Artie she was from another planet and he called her an idiot. As the film neared its exciting conclusion, Hester said she was hungry and devoured Artie. But it took her a dozen bites, not one as in the film.

Any Creature She Chose

she said she was blind
when she had eyesight
like the hungriest hawk
swooping down on its prey

she said she was deaf
when she had hearing
like an alert leopard
listening for night danger

she said she was crippled
when she had speed
like the swiftest gazelle
running from a heartless hunter

she said she could make him
turn into any creature she chose
gazelle or leopard perhaps
even a hawk forced to fly

he called her the worst liar
he called her a sinful deceiver
she paused and smiled
didn't say any more words
and he flew off frightened
to nowhere worth mentioning

As If This Is the Way of Things

A few minutes ago it was so cold, terribly, horribly cold, I have no other way to describe it, and now it is warm, too warm, and I have to discard my coat and gloves, need to unbutton my shirt in order to cope with this sudden heat. How can the temperature change so abruptly and drastically? I'd estimate the change of at least forty degrees Celsius in less than a minute. Perhaps a scientist or a meteorologist could explain it to me, but where could I find such a person walking down the street in an area of the city I am not familiar with?

Instead of the desired scientist or meteorologist, I pass on the street a tall, elongated person more female than male but with biceps bulging through a designer tank top and hair dyed the brightest red I'd ever seen. I wouldn't wager much if I had to say if this person is a woman or a man, my uncertainty is that great, but the biceps indicate a life of physical activity, of great strength.

Inexplicably, I want to ask if this person has ever read Sartre or Camus before or after the re-defining of redness, for I am certain the hair is dyed. I've never seen hair with such redness. I want to engage this person in conversation, in a friendly, ordinary, unthreatening way. Something in me says that if I can circumvent my shyness and usual social awkwardness, my life would take a turn for the better.

By the time I have my thoughts in a manageable order, the person is several dozen steps past me and I turn and hurry toward the person, more questions forming, estimating this uniqueness was closer to eight-feet tall than to a basketball centre's seven. I catch up with the striking walker, clear my throat, snap my fingers, contemplate doing a handstand but I'm inept at handstands, realizing that this might be one of those defining or seminal moments in my undefined existence.

The tall, gangling person turns toward me, glances downward, and I see the eyebrows are thick and darkly emerald, the teeth, though, are as white as for a TV commercial for magical whiteness. I notice other things as I walk along, jogging actually -- two strides of mine to one stride of the other -- straining to match the tall, gangling red-haired, emerald-eyebrowed, overly white-toothed stranger: a forehead scar the shape of a tiny full moon, four fingers on one hand and three on the other, one shoe of glistening gold and the other of shining silver-- how could I have missed these highlights before?

Now I have questions about music, films, geo-global politics, medicine, sports, even religion and the afterlife -- I want to probe the psyche, find out if we're compatible, in a platonic sense, of course.

We reach the outskirts of the city and as I'm finally ready to invite the person for drinks, my treat, I hear a noise stranger than the bright redness and the walker flies casually away as if this is the way of things and I'm left alone thirsty, lonely, but with a story that should make me more interesting to the next person I might chance to meet.

Foreplay

During his retirement party, the math teacher was talking to the attractive science teacher, and she told him about her dream of having sex with an adorable visitor from a recently discovered planet. Drink in hand, he told her that two days after a Saturday double-feature matinee, enthralled by The Attack of the 50-Foot Woman and The Incredible Shrinking Man, he sat in elementary-school class and wondered aloud what would happen if the Amazing 50-Foot Woman went out on a date with the Incredible Shrinking Man but the teacher kicked him out as if he had drawn the Amazing Woman and the Incredible Man naked in his notebook, passing it on to every student in that long-ago class, completely warping their expectations of lovemaking for a lifetime to come. Then the science teacher, finishing her third drink, asked the math teacher, "If I were a sexy space alien, would you go to bed with me?" In his excitement, nostalgic film musings, and incipient drunkenness, the math teacher failed to notice the tiny tentacles that were emerging from the back of the science teacher's long, lovely neck.

The Kafka Lovers

The man with a body
like Gregor Samsa's
and the woman
with a lost appetite
like the Hunger Artist's
both inventors of loneliness
both as isolated as sad planets
both caught by life's unfairness
met during a costume party
on the occasion of the release
from solitary confinement
of a man with the exact
neuroses and temperament
of Joseph K. just before
his inexplicable arrest.
The man with a body
like Gregor Samsa's
after a glass of wine
admits his desire
for the woman
with a lost appetite
like the Hunger Artist's
her simplicity and thinness
and unrepentant mysticism.
They exchange phone numbers
almost comprehend each other's
identity and perplexity
the fearful small talk
and frightened thinking
turning to the tactile
she stroking his shell
he touching her empty belly
like foreplay and enthrallment
during the beginning of madness
in an unwritten fairy-tale of love

by a ghost with a resemblance
to Kafka's romantic double.

Gluxoxgluxoxgluxoxgluxoxgluxox

At that moment, sitting in his car late on a warm summer's night and waiting for the light to change, he thinks of himself as the horniest and hungriest writer in the city. Horniness personified and hungriness on the loose, he smiles to himself. The light seems to be taking forever to change, and as he sits in his car, he jots down a few sentences about what he is thinking in a notebook he keeps on the dashboard in case the creative impulse hits him. Mr. Horny-Hungry as observer of the human condition, writer about life, and caught at a light that refuses to change. He realizes he is at an intersection of some literary significance (it had appeared in three novels and a few short stories he knows of) when a woman leans in his window and he thinks he has seen this in a hundred movies but cannot think of the title of one of them. He is expecting a clichéd proposition, something such as, You want a date, sweetie? or, You in the mood for a good time? or even, You looking for some hot action, honey? Instead she utters "Gluxoxgluxoxgluxoxgluxoxgluxox" and he thinks, What intersection am I really at? What city am I in? He hasn't travelled out of his home town in almost a decade; in fact, he has developed an aversion to travelling more than a few miles from his apartment, but he feels he has landed far-off, in an exotic country, finding there the most beautiful woman imaginable with a short skirt that exceeds all expectations. Her skirt rising even higher in miraculous display, repeatedly she utters "Gluxoxgluxoxgluxoxgluxoxgluxox." He has no idea what to say, something lustful or erudite, but he simply says that he is hungry and asks her if she would like to get a night-time meal with him, his treat, mentions his favourite eating place, and she says, "Erudition isn't called for tonight," as if she had read his mind. Suddenly he realizes that maybe she is observing him, preparing a report for someone, despite his note-taking, and he wants to voice authorial protest. He wants to take command of his thoughts and words, to get a story out of this unusual experience, yet the woman

41

resumes uttering "Gluxoxgluxoxgluxoxgluxoxgluxox" again and again. He takes out his wallet and offers the woman everything he has, not that he has much money, to leave him alone, and just then she smiles and he sees teeth a colour he can only describe as opulently burgundy. How could she have burgundy teeth, he thinks, and wants to write this in his notebook. He is afraid his car is turning into something else and fears he will be rearranged next -- it is, after all, she who seems to be observing him, her intense gaze impossible to describe, he decides, and all he can do is go along for the ride. Maybe they'll get something to eat later.

No One Believed She Was That Old

She wrote 500 erotic poems
in 500 years
of toil and hiding
relentless in imagining
the cruel magic
of the sensual
she admitted there were
unscrupulous exchanges
with malformed versions
of the demonic
how else could she describe
the perfection of madness
no one believed
she was that old
not 500 years
or appreciated what she wrote
except one lonely-shaped man
who craved affection
as much as immortality
and was willing to write
anything for anyone
even a malformed
collector of souls
standing nearby
where one enters sleep.

The Honeymoon's Over, Earthling

"How could you not pay for a round-trip travel package?" the android wife shouted at her human husband of two weeks.

"I thought the price was for a round-trip?" the husband apologized on the last day of their interplanetary honeymoon.

"We're stuck here."

"There are worse planets to be stuck on."

"We can't survive in the outside heat. If they kick us out of the climate-controlled hotel, we're history."

"I still love you."

"I hate your Earthling guts. If I ever get back to Earth, my next marriage will be to an android who knows how to plan a honeymoon."

The Oldest Profession Revisted

You want a sexy, everything included date?
I'm from the beyond, Mr. Horny Soul,
and I'll stroke every sensitive organ
and orifice and synapse you have
or can imagine, believe me,
a seductive otherworldly voice offers
enticing reminiscent salacious words
monotonous as broken yet beautiful watches.

Beyond what? the horny man wonders
measurements of confusion, disorientation,
and immeasurable distances from certainty
beyond the beyond.

He imagines a bright-eyed cheery-voiced ghost
with eternal sexual experience
love shaped as a tape measure
clutched in difficult to describe fingers.

Then the transaction is made
the currency and souls exchanged
one remains prosperous
the other shortchanged.

Divorce Proceedings

Ramona was resting on the floor of her residence on Xylor, a planet she had landed on a year ago. Looking through the skylight at Xylor's twin moons, she saw the face of her despicable husband on the smaller moon.

"The scary Man in the Moon," she said as co-astronaut Tobias entered the room.

"The Men in the Moons, you mean."

"I adore this planet."

"Departure time is soon."

"I'm staying, Tobias."

"If you don't leave today, you'll be stuck here forever."

"Less stressful than divorcing," she said, and visualized the numerous attentive appendages of her two beautiful Xylorian lovers.

As Was the Local Custom

Vexzolle the Magician, as was his professional name, appearing tired in human terms, sat cross-legged on the stage, lost in thought about his distant home, a planet that was just recently discovered by Earth astronomers. Even though he had been living among Earthlings in disguise for nearly fifty years (yet remarkably looked no older than an athletic thirty-year-old human). During those fifty years, Vexzolle sent reports once every Earth week back to his superiors about the Earthlings and their strange, puzzling ways. Any plans to colonize Earth in the future were contingent upon how well this first interplanetary "explorer" adapted to life on Earth.

Vexzolle, who was selected among his planet's more adventuresome inhabitants to be the first to not only visit Earth but to reside there indefinitely, had undergone numerous surgeries on his home planet in order to appear human, and was now wearing his Earthling magician's costume and an expression of anticipation despite his tiredness and what might be called disillusionment. Looking out at the audience, which included a local woman he had developed a fondness for and had even been contemplating mating with despite directives from his superiors against such physical interaction, Vexzolle suddenly smiled, a charming, engaging smile to which the audience reacted warmly. There wasn't even a word for smile on Vexzolle's home planet.

In his efforts to have a productive existence on Earth, to function on a daily basis as a performer, a magician who had travelled the world, Vexzolle had wholeheartedly mastered Earthling behaviour, emotions, and language. His career, which during its early years went beyond promising to illustrious, however, had descended through mishaps and miscalculation during the last decade into performing in community halls and school auditoriums, but Vexzolle believed that if he could pull off one big interplanetary trick he would be transformed from a has-been to his adopted planet's greatest magician. A few years ago, when he was impressing audiences with his magical skills and spellbinding performances, he was surprised to develop feelings of ambition, along with what Earthlings called an inflated ego. Yet in his efforts to become like the Earthlings, Vexzolle had also learned all too well human feelings of disappointment and unhappiness. Often in his weekly reports, he pondered and described these human emotions that could limit one's effectiveness as an efficient being, and which caused concern for his superiors.

Vexzolle, who hadn't gone a single day without missing his home planet as he attempted to make a life for himself on Earth, started to speak in his planet's language, words no one in the audience understood, but which translated loosely as "Take these Earthlings to a planet a million lifetimes from here..." He snapped his fingers as was the local custom, and the audience was amazingly emptied, not a single person left. Vexzolle's smile dissolved and he started to cry, an emotion he learned soon after arriving on Earth, realizing there was no one left to attest to his extraordinary interplanetary magic, including the Earth woman he had developed an affection for, and knew with an anguished pang of sadness that she would never be back to Earth. Despite his fifty years on Earth as a magician, both as a success and more recently as a failure, Vexzolle simply had not learned to reverse any of his spectacular tricks. His next report, Vexzolle sensed, would be full of sadness, an emotion he had attempted with much difficulty and little success to explain to his superiors on many other occasions.

L.K. Scott is a horror and mystery writer born in Sunnyside, Washington and for now lives in Solvang, California. He holds a BA in Screenwriting from Brooks Institute and has written, directed, and produced over a dozen films. When he's not writing you can find him tending to his garden, playing scary video games, or hunting down the best Mexican food around. To read more about L.K. Scott, visit him on his website titled Dreadful Notions and follow him on Twitter (@LKScott1) and Facebook.

The Beast of Hayvenhurst Manor
by L. K. Scott

On misty bogs that depress the Northwestern Cascades, which edge the Pacific denominated by seafarer brigands, where they always cast anchor and implored the protection of ankhs, incense, and hymns upon shore leave, there lined the woodland known as Stonybrooke. This name was given, we are told, by the thirsty souls of the adjacent village who linger in pubs and stray no further than the onerous paths allowed. Not far from this village, about ten or so miles, there lies a particularly silent mist-filled hollow. A shallow, slow creek eases through it, stagnant and thick in a dry summer and enlarged lavishly in a wet winter.

I had wandered one autumn afternoon when the grasses were orange and the leaves brown, the black bark of leafless branches my only shelter, mouldering earth and ice under my feet: conditions in which a man was quick to expire. Though many a year had passed since I trod the morose copse of Stonybrooke, I question should I not find the same frozen creek and the same decayed edifice of the ancient masonry home with large paired windows atop a mossy and fat frame which lorded over its sodden tuffet like a chub toad vigilant of imprudent prey.

In this nature, in some obscure point of history, came an itinerant man, a wistful gentleman who possessed extensible observations of the queer characteristics of society who had come for a constitutional at Hayvenhurst Manor, at the request of the manor's proprietor. He was a native of Montreal, so recognized for its cultural journalists and documentarians who supplied significant economical value. He was short, but lean with wide shoulders, long arms that swam in his loose-fitting, long-tailed coat, with hands that could've served as trowels and heavy black leather boots that anchored him deep in the marshland, and a blemished top hat adorned his mesocephalic head. His trousers, tight around his waist, wafted like flags at his narrow ankles, wet with particles of snow from the sparse patches along the primitive road. One may have mistaken him for a vagrant dressing above his class, yet he spoke as educated as a distinguished pedagogue and none but a dauntless man with issued purpose dared to wander so far in a biting winter's haze.

The young man introduced himself as Vivian Dubois, likely eighteen, but handsome, was well-nigh an ogre and should've been married proper with brutish young boys and poetic ingénues like a gentleman of his age, had kindly obliged me with an offer of escort to the nearest inn. I, who'd matched his kindness and vagrant inclinations, declined, for I had traversed the marshland before, inspired to capture charcoal drawings of the melancholy beauty of a country equinox. Then, as he wended his way through bog and steam, and black and orange woodlands and evergreen pines, through clumps of snow and dusty country trails, toward the manor, the surreal stillness of the afternoon fluttered his imagination with, no doubt, the haunted tales spewed from capacious mouths of village inhabitants. A sudden rustle of fieldfares rustled the gnarled thicket, but he continued, comforted by the songs in his own voice, learned from his explorations, to the manor where not even spiders ventured.

Vivian, with rose-red cheeks, arrived outside the stone path to Hayvenhurst Manor, whence he stopped to pluck a snowbell from its patch, the rarest of winter orchids, sinfully blue as a Mediterranean sky, pure enough to fill a brute with love and wonder.

Vivian climbed slowly up the cobblestone steps. His eyes were wide and eager, his skin pale and blemished with pink from the chill. As he approached the door, a shadow passed beyond the window, and there rose the sound of footfalls. Vivian looked at the bluebell and then he lifted the doorknocker as the door creaked open, and he found, looking into his eager eyes, a distinguished man, Master Esmund Howle. Tall and chivalrous he stood, but his face hid in shadows of the dimly lit hall cast his face pale.

Master Esmund Howle, the proprietor of the estate, had a soft foolish heart, tempting to the itinerant morsel who stood with a flower in hand, clad practically in rags on his stony porch. From the dirt of the earth grows beautiful creatures.

The master accepted the benefaction only with his eyes, never a hand, though he could not claim the same for the young man. They exchanged salutations informally, by first name.

Esmund, rough in his chivalrous manner, was intuitive by nature according to reasoners, traditions of yore, conscious of adversaries in moral society and for the last decade had been cognizant of a particular forbidden love. He'd been known as a scoundrel and blackguard, but for Vivian, who had known him intimately, was a playful woodland steed treasured more than a unicorn. He stood formidable before the doorway, burley and broad-shouldered, barrel-chested, with long luxurious hair the colour of dark Spanish chocolate, primed with eel oil, and stood erect and proper without unpleasant countenance despite his air of arrogance. He wore over his muscular frame charcoal coloured trousers that hugged his trunk-like legs and a midnight blue supercilious, yet stylish, bellamy shirt, which he wore casually unbuttoned to his naval, exposing his chest, hirsute as the dire wolf's coat and brawny as a plow horse.

The bluebell Esmund noted was a confession of Vivian's adoration. Vivian was never certain as to whether Esmund was famous or notorious within Stonybrooke, but Vivian believed Esmund relished in infamy. If an evening at a pub was disrupted by a brawl, or horses escaped from a pasture through a broken fence, Esmund was humorously and indirectly attributed and Vivian offered his own rectifiable assistance in the matter. They observed Esmund in awe, envy or riddle. In a shared pastime, Vivian was Esmund's object of uncouth gallantries, his amorous caressing as subtle as a bear in heat.

Esmund welcomed Vivian into his manor and stood, a gallant cock that patterned a husband, a warrior, and a fine gentleman that cawed in the pride of his heart more than his dwelling, glad for Vivian's presence. He smelled at once, with a rousing heart, the roasted and braised foul and felt the warmth of a fireplace from a room nearby that warmed the chill of his bones.

Esmund was a perfect picture, thriving contented in his liberal-hearted self. He was satisfied with his wealth, but not proud. There were many other things he'd rather be smug about, but rarely displayed his fancies. Esmund, Master Howle to most, as being exclusively the favorite by the locals of Stonybrooke, naturally, in their own interests, hardened themselves in humour at Esmund's chivalry and mischievous behavior, understood he could trample them with impunity, yet restrained. He was not boastful or dictating like the township's leaders and chose to live simply as his own master. There were, of course, within him, faults of insecurity.

The solitary Hayvenhurst Manor, both extravagant in size and modest in accoutrements, housed dusty and mildewed artifacts from the old kingdoms of Europe and Asia and sacred objects of African Tribesman. Esmund was not a traveler himself, and had likely obtained these relics from the sailors and adventurers who moored their ships at the seaside. To light the green fabric halls where excessive men would've chosen a dozen or more candles, Esmund found only six to be necessary. Though he could afford layers of tablecloths each table, one sufficed, and when the elite often required a dozen servants and cooks for a manor of a comparable size, Esmund adeptly looked after himself with perhaps only one or two to assist in meal preparation and minimal household work. From the dusty and fogged windows, the view stretched just beyond the iron fence entwined with woody stems of moonflowers and blackberries. The wretched weather affronted; distilled sunlight never came full to light and the dismal shadows consumed each room, darkest in the halls, stairwell and bedrooms. Hayvenhurst Manor, in general, had mostly wooden floors, sometimes stone, with clothed-covered walls of emerald green or royal purple and silver with woodsy luscious accents and crimson runners that would've appeared cheery and festive in spring or summertime when the air outside was hot and humid and the darkness inside offered a cool retreat, but now in the dreary later months, Vivian appeared a spectre among ubiquitous shadows, and indeed, that was the affect when summoned to dinner.

Bestowed upon him, a culinary abundance of scrumptious pig plumped with apple pudding in its belly, smoked cinnamon lamb and molasses horse, a side of baked foul folded snugly and tucked in a coverlet of pastry and swimming in onion sauce married cozily to cakes a vagrant man dared to consume with his greedy eyes: ginger cakes, soda cakes, chocolate cakes and loganberry crumble, apple pies and pumpkin pies with orange-honey and maple glazes. Vivian's mouth watered at the feast when a shadow lengthened over the table, and, upon looking to its source, saw the interloper, a youthful woman dressed in a Bernardina gown of rich golden dupioni and taffeta: a closely fitted bodice of creamy white and a square neckline that pressed her alabaster breasts up and a seductive velvety black V at the waist front. Her hair flowed in translucent curls, as golden yellow as her dress, skin like honey and milk, a porcelain face, round as a cat's and her sharp eyes, lit by candlelight, peered down like a malevolent golden queen in a blackened tower. Esmund introduced the woman as Sophia Collins, and they, to Vivian's despair, were to be married within a fortnight.

Vivian had traveled an ancient land to know a true Sphinx when he saw one. They were magical creatures, beautiful like summer ivy and just as poisonous, dominated jointly by society and religion. They were ancestors of Egypt mostly, sometimes Greece, impossible to rationalize with and tricksters by nature with alluring beauty; they required a lot of attention, and were confoundedly in the way sometimes.

Vivian would not have imagined, however, that one of those cruel potentates of above who joy in intolerance of the subjects below; on the contrary, the Sphinx administered justice with discrimination rather than love and verity, taking the burthen off the backs of queers and damned offering strength in reformation. A rod was passed in time and a Sphinx's claim of justice was only satisfied by inflicting portions to those in need of welcoming home and who sulked within traditional society to which the Sphinx claimed, "doing duty from above," and who chastised men with wandering eyes. Not a night passed among an urchin of respectable society who thanked her for freeing him of his illicit sexual burden, the craving for fellow men.

Vivian piqued himself upon his attraction to Esmund, a burden that he rather enjoyed, and had, for some decades, fathomed nestling in the master's bosom. He did not want, nor cared for the Sphinx's society life--not through dinner and evening, or weekend through a lifetime. Esmund arrested Vivian and the Sphinx's attention with an announcement. Indeed, he had invited Vivian for a proposal, one of connubial motives, however the proposal was not Vivian's, but for the Sphinx's. Vivian's eyes widened a bit before asserting control.

He, as gentle as his heart allowed, offered his blessings to Esmund and to the Sphinx then removed himself of their presence.

On that cold and brackish autumn's night, when a cloud possessed an ethereal moonlit glow and skeletal branches scraped the windowpane, Vivian retired to his bed alongside a lit, but drafty fireplace. The dark shadows of footsteps flickering by orange candlelight in a bluish night were stopped outside his bedroom door. Vivian had been reading when he shot upward after the door glided open and, illuminated by the candlelight, Esmund entered, clad in a black and scarlet silk robe that hung loosely from his body. Esmund closed the door behind him and intruded no further.

Vivian, nightly dressed in his tattered pyjamas rose to his feet clutching his blankets to his chest as though it would

56

conceal his offence.

"You must be mad," Vivian told him. His breath heaved, but his eyes never strayed from Master Howle.

"I am in the grip of madness," he said. His voice was rough as it was velvety, conscious of the Sphinx fast asleep in a nearby room.

Vivian stepped forward around the bed, chin high, tight lipped. "Leave at once," he said, "and I'll say nothing of what has happened here."

"You won't say anything of the sorts," Esmund stepped closer. "I recollect you're here on my invitation."

"I'll sleep outside then."

Esmund took another step closer, his voice even softer. "You'll do no such thing."

Vivian advanced a step too. He fidgeted with the blanket and eyed the door. "I'll ring the bell."

If Esmund's stoic countenance were capable of forming a smile, he would've done so. "Who would come at this hour? And would you really let a servant find a man in your bedroom at this hour?"

"I don't care about other men," said Vivian. "Do you have any idea what you're asking? You'll be ruined if anyone ever found out we had this conversation. What would Sophia say? You're getting married."

Esmund diverted his gaze. "Not for a fortnight," he said.

"You're not a virgin for your fiancé," Vivian reminded him.

"I know," Esmund responded with a light chuckle, "We were both there. I'm afraid a union like ours would be frowned on in my town."

"The world is changing," Vivian said. "People are talking of wars and revolution, rights for women and freedom from slavery. The world for us is changing."

"I agree, Vivian. The world is liberating, but not fast enough, and not in our time. I can't justify a reason for you to become a social pariah because of my irrefutable advancements on you, which is why I'm marrying Sophia.

She can free us of this burden."

"I didn't realize I was such a burden."

"I respect you which is why I believe you should hear it from me. In person we can have a proper goodbye and tomorrow we can be saved. We'll finally lead society lives again. We'll have no secrets to hide." Esmund took Vivian by the hand. "I'm sorry if my invitation lead you to believe something more."

"It's just as well," said Vivian, relinquishing his hand. "A gull may love a toad, but where would they nest?"

Never having been called a toad, Esmund flinched. He held Vivian's chin.

"With a bit of imagination, a toad can fly too." Master Howle said and pressed his lips against Vivian's neck.

Vivian suddenly felt himself drifting through the air, light as a gull's feather, to the luxurious bed proceeded by the weight of Esmund's solid body on top of his. Their tongues indulged in a trilby and gave vent to their surplus of syncopated passion, a measure before the cotillion of Esmund's fervent erection, sized like a leather billy club, fretting against Vivian's waist.

"I cannot be lead on, if this is what you think I am, Master Howle--" Vivian could hardly utter a stave, his hips betrayed his words.

Upon hearing his name spoken so formally by such a dear friend and lover, Esmund pulled back. "Oh, my darling," Esmund said as he freed them of clothing, "if only for once more, trust me."

Vivian tilted his head so that his lips brushed against Esmund's, parted his legs, and urged him inside.

The candlelight burned low while Vivian fell asleep dandled in Esmund's perspired embrace.

Esmund stayed longer, until a quarter past one, when he was certain Vivian would not stir upon retreat. He delicately brushed a strand of hair off Vivian's face and allowed his fingertips to brush against his cheek, for a moment too long, long enough for Esmund's heart to prance like the flickering orange light across his lover's face.

Unostentatiously, Esmund slipped out of Vivian's bed. He carried with him a vial of the viscous fluid, the sacred elixir to all human life. He gathered his robe and crept back to his room where he covered his naked body with thick wools that even the chilly night's air could not permeate.

Through the manor, Esmund, shrouded in a hood and cloak, drifted by candlelight along the corridor, down the creaky staircase and slipped out the back door into the dead of night. Hoary grey moonlight from low overcast silhouetted black oaks with branches gnarled like an ancient sailors fingers, crooked with arthritis. The frigid air smelled nearing of winter and the spice of decomposed pine needles and swamp matter. A suffocating and motionless vapor clutched the marshland where the stony path from the manor ended and the marshland began. Ancestral gravestones jutted from the tar-like earth adjacent to a bramble patch, obstacles that subverted his pace and snagged at his clothing. At the final row of graves where the last glow of moonlight was suffocated by darkness and the only sound was the blood throbbing in his ears he met Sophia draped in white and gold. Her outstretched arm, raised not even by a goose pimple in the icy chill, carried an unnatural hue.

Esmund handed her the vial.

"His and only his," Sophia said.

"As you instructed."

She reached for his wrist. He turned his palm so that it faced what remained of the moonlight. In his hand, she uncorked the vial. The contents gathered in his palm, dripped through his splayed fingers. Like a caterpillar breaking through its cocoon, she slipped from her gown. His hands explored her breasts.

"Free me," Esmund whispered.

Unaffected by the cold, she guided his hands down her

body, to the hair between her legs, and to her feet in the marsh. She spoke, just above a whisper, to the earth and sky.

"As the snail that creeps from the shell was turned eftsoons into a toad, and thereby was forced to make a stool to sit on; so the traveler that straggled from his own country is in short of time transformed into such a shape, that he is faine to alter his mansion with his manners, and to live where he can, not where he would."

Esmund slept beside a dying fire that night and woke in the early hours of morning, cold as death, his head aching so that he cried out in pain when he moved. All around him everything appeared the same, no remedies from Sophia and still, the one thing he cared for, with heartfelt interest, was still crusted between his fingers as it had been all night.

Boar folded into pastry with cinnamon apple preserves, a side of eggs with bacon, and a wedge of cheese was served at the breakfast table where Esmund had expected to see his fiancé and his lover. He arrived to find Sophia sipping on tea, alone. Vivian, she had told him, had not been sighted from his room since the night before and Esmund thought it uncharacteristic of the itinerant young man to discount himself from such a feast. Sophia's aversion was unmatched by Esmund's unease and took issue upon the matter himself. Journeying could be quite stressful and perhaps he had taken ill. Furthermore, he was eager to attest Sophia's charm for if he could be near Vivian without unquenchable desire, they would finally be free. Free of transgression, free from love.

Three sturdy knocks and not a stir. Upon opening Vivian's door, he first saw the red across the floor, soaked in the carpets. The mound on the floor he had at first mistaken for a linen was a bloody skin.

Esmund was not a fainting man, but he could have right then. An icy morning breeze flowed from an open window across the room and caught his breath. On the sill were the gashes, claw marks from a beast unlike any Esmund had known.

On unsteady feet, he sprinted from the corridor and

down the stairs of the main hall to the back door beneath the room where Vivian had been staying. On the footpath, more claw marks embedded in the soggy earth made way to the woods. Esmund screamed for Vivian, but only the soughing pines replied.

"You are free now," said Sophia who appeared behind him. "For who could love a monster?"

He demanded from the sphinx a cure but love was not a curable affliction, for it was not an illness. When she could not bring Vivian back, Esmund was left face to face with his own reflection in the window where his breath misted the glass. Outside, rain broke the clouds.

Esmund wasted no thoughts on his gentlemen etiquette or the pride that cawed in his heart more than his dwelling, for from his heart he had betrayed, he could no longer see himself as a gentleman, warrior, or husband. His home, that he had once cherished, was a strange unwelcoming institution. "I won't go! I cannot leave him!" To the cadence of some meaningless refrain, he found his way to his bedroom, fumbling with the lock and the click of the key as it turned.

He stood darkly at the window, lord of his estate and the marshland and the woods and the beast that lived there, more frightened by the monsters that inhabited the manor. A well-trained footman had laid out the trivial arrangement of the morning on his bed; an earthenware coffee pot sat at the table beside a fire, the embers already dying under the velvet of charcoal and ash. Esmund removed the decorative golden rope that adorned the bed used to draw the heavy curtains around the canopy and placed it on the table beside the coffee-pot and paused at the snowbell, it seemed more sinfully blue than yesterday. He listened to the faint, far away sounds of something howling, sharp as a wolf and bigger than a bear permeating the woods.

"All I have is this," he said inwardly. "I had more, perhaps a good deal. I found him again, in my bed, only to lose him again forever. How much longer could this go on?" Knowing this as he did, he suddenly wanted to cry out.

He braced himself against the window and wondered what would be left of him. His risk was negligible and he loved Vivian above all others and Vivian's consolation was no less than torture. He'd never dream of them together. Yet Esmund couldn't bear to part from his home and the woods where Vivian was exiled. There was no place in the world he could occupy where the people wouldn't talk of the monster in the woods, but to Esmund, Vivian would always be his soul mate.

Esmund checked the clock on the mantle. A quarter to noon. The sphinx wouldn't be back to check on him for another few hours.

Hours. A lifetime, all the same. In a fortnight, where would he be? A monster worse than the one a villager would hunt with torches and guns and chains. He lifted beseeching eyes to his favorite flower unable to prevent his muscles from contracting like a man who aches to jump but lacks courage.

He worked a groan from his throat, repeating over and over again, "Vivian," but fell silent. He did not need a chant to pick up the bed rope and hoist it over the sturdy beam from his bedpost. He experimented the height and sturdiness of the rope and with his right hand he slipped the loop over himself so that it rested around his neck. At once Esmund felt illness from his stomach and if he did not make haste, he would grow weak and fall back to the bed which would thump and alert the servants and the sphinx. So he hurried, whimpering as he completed his task and felt nothing more than the falling of his body and the abrupt tightness of rope around his neck.

It's been many a year since I had last stood at the marshes of Hayvenhurst and the preceding tale is given, almost in these precise words, in Stonybrooke that remains a village today much as it was then. There you'll find pleasant, however dreary, narrators, I suspect to be poor, in shabby clothing with salt-and-peppered hair who make an effort to be entertaining. The unfortunate souls who find themselves in the midst of their journey stopping for respite and a swig at the local pubs on foggy nights will turn doubt over in their mind, puzzled by the ratiocination of the narrative. When their mirth subsides and the silence of night restores, the local patrons are left with contemplation of their sons and daughters and husbands and wives who had throughout the years ventured into the marshes and almost never return. The few who come back frostbitten with missing shoes, torn clothes, and bodies close to death, shriek with audacious tales of the beast in the woods and the sphinx, who watches from the upstairs window, forever trapped alone inside.

Trent Roman is a writer from Montreal with an interest in all types of fiction strange and unusual. He is fascinated by what makes people tick at both the intimately personal level and the sweeping societal level. He is currently pursuing a PhD in Literature, focused on disaster and the environment. His work has appeared in a number of independent press venues; a list, and updates on new projects, can be found on his blog at trentroman.wordpress.com.

Riven
by Trent Roman

The October sky had split asunder several hours ago and showed no sign of relenting, rain pouring down in thick solid sheets. Sarah watched it spatter against the street and sidewalks, though she herself was warm and dry beyond the glass panes of The Isle of Java. The tall cappuccino in front of her had grown tepid since Sarah and Olivia had sought refuge from the downpour in the off-campus shop.

"Sarah agrees with me -- right, Sarah?"

Sarah blinked and forced herself to focus back on her fellow climatic refugees. Olivia was looking at her expectantly, as were the two other women, whose names she could not recall. They were undergrads, students in one of the Gender Issues classes where Olivia was working as a teaching assistant.

"I'm sorry," she admitted, "I guess I spaced out there. What were we talking about?"

"Ah, it's not important," Olivia waved it off. "I think we've drifted quite a ways off from the original topic, which was the mid-term, yeah?"

One of the students nodded and started asking questions on the format of the exam, and Sarah tuned the conversation out once more. She had not taken on a teaching assistant position of her own this semester to focus on her research and was feeling oddly disconnected from the various debates that inevitably started whenever scholars gathered. In fact, she'd been feeling distracted generally, never really at ease except for when she lost herself in the depths of her ever-growing thesis. She was studying the influence of the old, pre-Abrahamic nature religions on the Torah, trying to identify remnants of those old faiths in the Jewish holy text. Her advisor was pleased with the progress she was making, and she was well on schedule to deliver her dissertation.

Her personal life was also going well -- she'd been with Olivia for eight months now, and their relationship had reached a level of steady comfort without stultifying into routine. So she was at a loss to identify a source for this malaise that loomed over her recently, as surely as the dark clouds hung heavily in the sky outside.

Sarah bit back a sigh, not wishing to appear even more melancholy than she was already revealing, and turned to face the grey light lounging against the glass windows. The Isle of Java was just next to Chasm City College, where the still-green campus gave way to the usual streets and shops of a major metropolitan city. Across the way, blinking in and out of view as cars whizzed by, were signs for a chain bookstore, a small thrift clothing shop and part of a Thai restaurant. The portrait was completed by an old woman, tall but stooped, bundled in many layers of clothes which even the thrift shop would surely snub. One of the city's silent army of vagrants, Sarah concluded, although this one seemed to have misplaced the cart or knapsack in which they held their few precious possessions.

The woman stood in the rain, making no effort to try and seek shelter under the parapet of the restaurant, water visibly dripping from knotty white hair. She was staring across the street, just as Sarah was, her gaze (Sarah was surprised to find that, despite the distance, she could make out deep azure irises) locked on the Isle's frontispiece. Sarah could only imagine that the old hobo was thinking about the warmth inside the café, contemplating whether a few minutes of comfort would be worth the humiliation of being chased away by a clerk when it became clear that she had no means of buying anything.

Suddenly seized by a violent sense of injustice, Sarah rose from her bench, determined not to let this pass without action, as she had so many times in the past. She would go to the tramp and invite her into the shop, give her whatever she needed to pay for a cup of something warm, and make sure the clerks kept their distance.

Unfortunately, in her resolve, she'd forgotten that she was sharing her booth bench with one of Olivia's students, and had the inner seat. The poor girl, startled by Sarah's sudden motion, tried to quickly move out of the way but didn't quite manage to get her knees clear of the table and stumbled in a crouch to the floor.

"Steady on!" Olivia exclaimed, looking at her with consternation. Sarah, mortified, reached over to help the student back to her feet. To make matters worse, the girl, still looking bewildered, was babbling a string of apologies, as though this debacle had somehow been her doing.

"No, no, I'm sorry," Sarah insisted. "Totally my fault. I just -- I forgot where I was for a moment. Really, just stupid. There's this old woman, see, and I thought--"

Sarah had turned to point out the window towards the tramp, but to her surprise the previously immobile itinerant had lived up to the term and moved away. More embarrassed than ever, Sarah shook her head and brushed off some dirt from the student's coat.

"Well, there was a woman," she said with a tight, contrite smile.

Olivia reached across the table and gingerly prodded Sarah's cappuccino. She looked back up with an expression of tolerant exasperation.

"I'm thinking decaf, yeah?"

At first, Sarah wasn't quite sure where she was. The sky was a burning red dome as the sun kissed the distant horizon, the hot, arid desert air still hung heavily on her shoulders. Yellow plateau and white sand stretched as far as the eye could see, punctuated only by other, lesser rocky outcroppings -- and the glittering crescent of the Roman legions. The sight of the besieging army caused memory to come crashing back down into her consciousness, weighing her down further. It was the same nightmare she had been awakening to for the last several weeks: Masada.

The unrelenting heat must have caused her to black out for a moment -- it wouldn't have been the first time she'd succumbed to the harsh conditions in the fortress since they had been forced out of Jerusalem. The food and water the men had obtained during the last raid against a nearby village was all but spent. She was hungry and thirsty all the time, and had nothing with which to quell the cries of the children, similarly afflicted.

Sarah stared down at the gathered soldiers waiting at the bottom of the ramp they were constructing, raising her hand to shield her eyes from the reflecting glare. They ambulated far below, building to their inevitable victory. Sarah watched them for a few minutes when her attention was caught by a figure not shining but billowing. At the feet of the ramp stood a woman clad in the ceremonial robes of a priestess of Diana. She seemed youthful, elegant, and stared up at the fortress in apparent defiance. Sarah couldn't fathom why she was here -- Diana was not a patron of the legions, and Masada was, as she would gladly testify, no place for a woman.

As she looked down, Sarah caught the distinct impression of two blue orbs. The woman's eyes? No; that was impossible, not at this distance. A pair of sapphire earrings sparkling in the light, in all likelihood. Their pitiless glint gave Sarah a chill, and she turned away from the ramparts.

Sarah ambled back to the archway she had adopted as her temporary home in the fortress and settled against the hard stone. It occurred to her that she should search for the children, make sure they at least had a little something to eat, but she couldn't summon the will to make the effort. She lay there, despondent, until her husband came running into view, and Sarah pulled back even further into her alcove, trying in vain to hide.

How she had wept when her father had married her off

to Eleazar ben Matthias, that hard stranger from the north! She had known then that it would end poorly for her, an impression confirmed when her husband had joined first the Zealots and then the Sicarii. Secretly, she had been glad when he and his fellow 'warriors' were chased out of Jerusalem by the Romans; at last, it seemed, she would have some peace. Without her domineering husband, she had ventured out further and further, forging friendships with many of the local market women -- in particular, an Egyptian woman who sold charms and told her much about the mystic ways of her people.

But then had come news of the Sicarii's continuing depredations, even against fellow Jews, and Sarah found herself turned out by the lawmakers in Jerusalem, condemned to join her husband in whatever doom he had brought down upon himself. It seemed that fate was now near at hand: Eleazar had his dagger drawn, and his face was frantic with worry.

"The Romans will attack!" he declared to her. "The fortress will fall, and if we do nothing we shall all perish under their swords -- or worse, become their slaves. We have decided: we will rob the oppressors of their victory by dying first."

"What?" Sarah stammered. "What are you saying?"

"To kill ourselves would be a sin, but if we kill each other to deliver each other, we shall join with Yahweh and the righteous martyrs who passed before us. Come, quickly; I want to make sure there are brothers left still to kill me once this is done."

"You're mad!" Sarah cried, shying away. "I will not die for you or your Lord. I have the children to take care of, they need me--"

"I have already delivered the children," Eleazar said, and Sarah was horrified to see, now that he was closer, that his dagger and tunic was stained with fresh blood. "Don't make this any more difficult than it needs to be, woman."

Crushed by grief and horror, Sarah could muster no

defence as he grabbed her by the back of her robes, restraining her. The hand holding the dagger plunged in a quick, vicious arc into her stomach. Sarah screamed as she felt the metal bite into her flesh, kicking to free herself from the weight of the robes. She felt them give, felt light, and leapt up, only to miss the floor by half-a-meter and go tumbling face-first from the bed.

There was a gasp behind her, but Sarah ignored it, forcing herself to her feet and pushing forward. She saw the doorway to the bathroom and clumsily angled for it, even as Olivia called out after her: "Sarah! What the bloody hell?"

Out of instinct she flicked the light switch, flooding the small bathroom with harsh, white fluorescence. Sarah stopped, leaning against the counter, looking at her panting reflection in the mirror. There was no fortress, no husband or children. There was only a panicky young woman, trembling in her underwear. Then there were two as Olivia joined her in the bathroom.

"What's wrong? What's happened?"

"Nothing," Sarah said, then realizing that clearly wouldn't do, added: "It was just a nightmare. I -- I got confused, that's all. Sorry I woke you up."

"Must have been one stupendous nightmare," Olivia said, her voice both groggy and irritated. "The way you were screaming, I'm sure somebody in the building must have called the fuzz."

"Sorry," Sarah said again. She ran water from the tap, cupped her hands and splashed it across her face.

Olivia relaxed and took a more conciliatory tone. "Want to talk about it?"

"Not really," Sarah said, and then went on to describe her dream anyway.

"That certainly qualifies for kicking and screaming," Olivia said afterwards, slipping her arms around Sarah's waist and resting her chin on Sarah's right shoulder. "This massacre -- real or dreamland?"

"Oh, Masada was very real. My father used to tell my

brother and me stories about it when we were kids. He'd sit in his chair in the evening, point his finger at us while we were lying on the floor, listening, and make us promise never to forget about any of the lost, from Masada to the Holocaust."

Olivia gave a shudder. "Not quite Mother Goose."

"No -- I had nightmares about it when I was a kid too. Sometimes I'd lie in bed after he'd kissed us good-night, totally awake, wondering if, were it all to happen again, as he often feared it might, whether my father would be the one to kill me."

"There's no-one like parents to fuck you up, is there?" Olivia said after a moment.

"No," Sarah agreed, and fell silent, just enjoying the warmth of Olivia on her back and the support radiating from the other woman. She stared at her own troubled reflection, trying to make sense of what was happening behind those sleep-clouded blue eyes.

Obviously she had dredged up the memory of the fortress from those same childhood nightmares, but she couldn't understand why it should surface now. She wasn't feeling besieged or trapped by anything. She'd recognized the so-called priestess figure in the dream as the tramp she'd seen earlier and assumed there was some guilt at work for not having helped the vagabond, but enough to merit that level of self-violence? She supposed it all went back to that same ineffable malaise that had been haunting her of late, though she still didn't have a clue as to what the source might be.

And, looking at her own haggard reflection, she wondered if she really wanted to know.

Sarah felt distracted as she worked on her bibliography in the quietly intense atmosphere of The Isle of Java in mid-afternoon. Her attention kept drifting away from the flicker-glow of the laptop before her towards the windows, and the streetscape beyond. If she were to be honest with herself, Sarah had to admit she was looking for someone: the old woman of the day before. She remembered her undergraduate psychology classes well enough to know that she was displacing the real cause of her disquiet onto a problem that could be solved. But knowing didn't banish the feeling, and Sarah continued to hope that the tramp might present herself, so that Sarah could invite her in, give her some food, talk to her a little -- at the very least, find out her name.

"Lilith."

Sarah jumped, startled by the sudden intrusion of a voice into her thoughts, and turned to face Olivia. "What?"

"Lilith," Olivia said again, thrusting an open book at her. "This is a painting of her one of my Women's Issues in Art History students brought to conference earlier. She's one of the characters you're studying for your project, yeah?"

"She is," Sarah agreed, looking at the painting. She'd seen it before in her studies, of course: a late nineteenth century piece by John Collier, it showed a fair, naked woman with fiery orange hair in a forest, caressing a large snake sensuously wrapped about her. The figure it claimed to portray, Lilith, was one of the salient thrusts of her thesis. Although recent stories in the Judeo-Christian tradition often identified her as Adam's first wife, many researchers had been able to trace Lilith back to pagan roots in the ancient Mesopotamian pantheon of demigods. Tracing Lilith's gradual inclusion into early Hebraic lore as a demonic entity was a case-in-point example of the pagan/Jewish 'borrowing' she was trying to bring to light.

"I thought she was supposed to be some kind of proto-feminist," Olivia said. "But a snake doesn't speak to the feminine aspect; you know what I mean?"

"She's popular with feminists because of a medieval story about how she was kicked out of Eden for refusing to lie under Adam when they had sex. But other stories say she later became the mother of all demons, and a consort of Satan -- the snake."

"Shagging a snake," Olivia shook her head. "No thanks."

Sarah nodded in agreement and pushed the book back towards Olivia before turning back to her papers. The other woman looked at it, her expression one of disappointment. Sarah frowned.

"What's wrong?"

"Nothing, nothing at all," Olivia said, taking the book and stuffing it -- rather brusquely -- into her bag. "Don't let me bother you."

Sarah suddenly understood. She had told herself that Olivia might tire of her distraction, and it was beginning to happen. The book had been an attempt to reach out to her through her research, one of the few areas where she was still capable of mustering genuine passion. And she had casually rebuffed the entreaty instead of seizing it as an opportunity to connect again.

"Look, Olivia..." Sarah started, searching for the right words to explain and apologize. Her eyes strayed to the window, and Sarah suddenly shot up from her seat and crab-stepped out of the booth. "I'll be right back; don't go anywhere!"

Olivia's sigh was lost to Sarah as she made for the door and stepped out onto the sidewalk. It took her a few moments to spot the waddling figure down the street. It was the hobo of the other day, Sarah was sure of it: she had looked up to find the tramp staring into the café window again, and immediately recognized the azure eyes.

Sarah dodged her way around the pedestrian traffic, her sights set firmly on the ambulating bundle of ragged clothes in front of her. She called out, but without a name, she knew that she had little chance of catching the attention of someone accustomed to being ignored. Sarah caught a brief glance of the old woman's face as she turned a corner and bit back a curse. It was irrational, it was illogical, but for whatever reason she was suddenly convinced that as soon as she turned the corner herself, the tramp would be...

Gone. No sign of her. Just the same city crowd as the

street she had just left. Sarah started looking about for a side alleyway or an open shop the vagabond might have ducked into, but nothing suggested itself as a good possibility.

Sarah couldn't fathom where the tramp had vanished, nor could she explain her previous certainty -- borne out -- that the old woman would disappear. Dispirited and confused, Sarah turned back around towards the Isle, knowing that these events would do little but add to her disquiet... and that she had a lot more apologizing to do now.

The night air was warm despite the chilly weather announcing the onset of winter. This was because of the fires, burning hot all around Sarah as pyres were lit by the enthusiastically jeering crowd that had turned up for the auto de fé. Her view of the perversely festive proceedings was better than she would have liked, as she was one of those tied to the stakes arrayed along the docks. Hay had been piled beneath her, as it had those to her right and left, in case the small wooden platform she currently stood on didn't burn well enough.

She had given up on pleading her innocence or crying for aid and mercy after screaming herself hoarse in the opening hours of the mass execution. She had even run out of tears, as though the heat had already evaporated what water her body had to spare. She felt hollowed-out, incapable of feeling anything but a distant sense of despair and finality.

The Inquisitorial judges in their red or black robes were moving at a slow and steady pace through the crowd, as if there was any semblance of dignity to be maintained in this carnival of slaughter. They had started at the other end of the docks, leaving Sarah to anguish for hours on her stake until she felt as she did now, numb in body, mind and spirit. When they finally filed up in front of her pyre, Sarah didn't even bother to look up at them, her chin resting on her chest.

One of the clerics read off her name, place of residence,

and ancestry. Then he launched into the list of crimes she had been accused and found guilty of. Most the charges were nothing short of fanciful, but they had enough evidence to back up the prime allegations, her refusal to convert and dabbling in witchcraft, that the rest was simply decorative propaganda.

Sarah had tried to tell them during her 'trial' that the minor rituals she'd become involved in where not wicked, but spells aimed at protecting loved ones and ensuring good health. But even if they had been inclined to believe that, the Moorish girl who'd introduced Sarah to white magic had been arrested several days ago as part of Queen Isabella's campaign against the Moors, and had apparently confessed to hideous deeds under torture, naming Sarah as an accomplice and revealing that Sarah continued to practice her Jewish faith in secret.

After the recitation was done, one the priests asked if she had something to say in her defence. This was such a preposterous question that Sarah finally looked up at them, hoping her expression could still muster some of the contempt she felt for them, though she remained tight-lipped. Most the clerics were stoned-faced with counterfeit solemnity or, more honestly, smiling grim little smiles as they returned her glare. There was only one woman among their number, a nun from her habit, with a matronly shape and mien. She was the only one not looking at Sarah; her head was bowed, the expression beneath her was wimple shamed and resigned. Her deep blue eyes flashed up for a moment and met Sarah's, but they dropped back to the ground a moment later. Sarah couldn't care less. She would have spat in all their faces had she any saliva left between the screaming and the heat.

Eventually the priests tired of waiting for her to beg or rail or at them, and indicated to the hooded executioners to light the pyre. The dry straw caught quickly, and soon high flames snaked into the air, dancing about her as the smoke choked her and the heat seemed to boil her alive. Despite her prior conviction that she had no more voice to cry out with, she was soon screaming again as the flames began eating their way through the small wooden platform, licking at her feet. Within seconds the burlap robes in which she had been dressed had caught fire as well, and Sarah was bound by flame.

Then, suddenly, her burning clothes were ripped off her, her bindings broken, and she was thrown from the platform and to the hard ground. She tried to roll, the impression of heat still stinging her skin, but a new figure loomed over her and restrained her, holding down each of her wrists. It was a dark-skinned woman with broad, worried features, and for a moment Sarah thought her Moorish friend had somehow returned from the dead. Then she realized that it actually was--

"Olivia?"

"Goddess, you gave me a scare," Olivia said, letting go of her wrists. "You were screaming again, fighting with the sheets..."

Sarah blinked several times in succession, trying to dispel the confusion tumbling about her mind. Above her was the bedroom ceiling, to her side the bed, down past her feet a tangled mass of blankets.

"I had another nightmare," Sarah said at length.

"No kidding."

Sarah sat up, and because it had helped last time, told Olivia about the dream.

"You know, Sarah..." Olivia said, her expression serious, after Sarah had finished. "It's one thing to have a really bad nightmare every so often. Two in as many days..."

"It's nothing," Sarah said.

"It's not nothing," Olivia insisted. "And it's not just the nightmares, either. You've been really distracted the last few weeks."

Sarah sighed and let her head drop back to the floor. "I know. I feel... odd, like I'm constantly waiting for something to happen, but I don't know what that is."

"Maybe you should see somebody about it."

Sarah sat up quickly. "I'm not crazy."

"No, of course not," Olivia said, holding her hands up. "I'm just saying that you might benefit from professional advice."

Sarah -- whose dreams were haunted by a vagabond woman who appeared to vanish into thin air -- decided that seeing professionals was the last thing she needed. Because they might actually find something, and she didn't think she could cope with that on top of everything else.

"Look, I'll make you a promise," Sarah said. "I'm going to take the rest of the week off. I'll go to class, but the research and the thesis can wait. I'm ahead of schedule, so I can afford take a break. No more worrying about old religions for a while -- it'll be just you and me when we're together. And if I have any more screaming nightmares... then I'll go see someone. Deal?"

Olivia sighed, but smiled affectionately, her expression stating that she just couldn't stay upset with Sarah. "Deal," she said.

As they embraced on the bedroom floor, Sarah hoped she wouldn't have cause to recant her promise -- and in particular, that the blue-eyed woman would be banished from her dreams and waking hours both.

Taking a brief sabbatical from her research had proved an able solution: although the generalized sense of malaise persisted, Sarah was no longer tormented by dreams or waking visions (as she was now convinced the old vagabond woman had been). Her attention still wanted to stray, but Sarah was able to tame it. Eventually, however, she needed to decide whether to extend her sabbatical indefinitely and risk her degree or get back to work. Sarah and Olivia had agreed that it would be better return to her studies, though watchful for any more problems. Sarah had no idea what she would do if the nightmares did return, but she firmly kept her mind from pursuing that line of thought.

After polishing her bibliography and proofing what she'd already written provoked no new attacks, Sarah resolved that it was time to seriously hit the books once more. Since Olivia was busy correcting mid-terms that Friday evening, Sarah decided to go out to the Simon Wiesenthal Memorial Library, the best repository of Hebraic lore in all Chasm City. The library was closed to the public on weeknights, but the curator was a friend and had agreed to loan her a key to do her research during off-hours. Sarah preferred going when the place was otherwise empty; not just for the absolute quiet, but for the sense of communion that came from being alone with the books.

Sarah let herself in, barred the door behind her, and dropped her bag on a nearby table. She booted up a computer, called up the books she wanted and sat down with a pile to read through. Time began to slip by unnoticed as she immersed herself in her work.

Sarah was startled out of her focus by the sudden sound of breaking glass as a nearby window exploded inwards in a hail of shards. Adrenaline surged through her and made time slow down enough for her to make out the shape of the bottle in the middle of the tempest of glass, one end trailing sickly, oily flame from the rag stuffed into the aperture. The Molotov cocktail detonated as it hit the floor, but instinct had kicked in and Sarah was already motion, throwing herself to the floor behind the heavy table. All at once, the library filled with a reddish glow, a wave of heat washed over her skin, and she heard a crackling roar even over the sound of her own heartbeat beating at her eardrums. For a moment she was frozen in terror, eyes wide and scanning in a jerky fashion, half-expecting something else to jump out at her. Sarah only pushed herself away from the table when she saw that one of the bookcases had caught fire, the flames already spreading to its neighbours. The burning paper was spreading thick, black smoke which burnt at her eyes and left an acrid taste in her mouth.

Sarah was able to master herself long enough to grab her bag off the table. She cast a regretful look at the books she was abandoning, stuffed several of the heavy tomes into her bag and ran for the door. When she burst out onto the street, her stinging eyes missed the fact that there were a few steps to the ground and she stumbled. She sprawled onto the ground, scraping her knees on the concrete sidewalk. She didn't get up right away, taking advantage of the fresh air to finally let out the series of coughs that had been building in her lungs from the smoke.

"What's this? I think I've smoked out a rat."

The voice was male, young and snidely contemptible. Sarah felt a chill, certain what she would find as she looked up. He was white and shaved almost bald, wearing a white t-shirt, ragged black jeans and a leather jacket despite the heat. A chain piercing hung from his left nostril to his ear and brass rings pierced his eyebrows. There was no doubt it was him who had thrown the firebomb. He approached her, his pace slow and menacing, clearly aiming to intimidate and -- to lone, weaponless Sarah -- succeeding.

"Just when you think the night can't get any better," he said, grinning cruelly.

Sarah cast about for an escape route, but her back was to the burning library, and judging by his lean physique, he would probably be able to catch her if she ran. As she was looking, however, her eyes happened on a figure in the shadows across the street--hunched and ragged, but with blue eyes that glittered in the darkness.

"Hey!" the skinhead called out, stepping in front of her. "Look at me when I'm talking to you, bitch. What, you think somebody's going to help you? I don't see any pigs, do you? No, you're mine... but I promise I'll go easy on you, if you make me happy first."

He reached down and undid the fly of his jeans. The sound of the zipper acted as a trigger for Sarah, who sprang up off her knees, swinging her bag up and around. The bag and the heavy books within collided sharply with the skinhead's face, and Sarah heard something crunch even as the neo-Nazi's head was whipped around in a spray of blood. He staggered away, screaming and holding on to his face with both hands.

Sarah was about to break into a run, but the skin recovered fast, spinning himself around and back into her path.

"You boke by bose!" He spat, saliva thick with blood. "I godda gill you, bitch!"

The skin reached into his jacket and pulled out a switchblade, flipping it open. He was more cautious this time, moving slowly, one arm out to deflect a potential blow from her bag even as the other was ready to thrust with the blade. Then a pair of grimy hands jutted from behind him, grabbing on to his head and chest, and twisted. Violently. There was a sharp crack and the skin collapsed to the ground, lifeless. Behind him, the blue-eyed vagabond regarded her handiwork with a harsh smile. The tramp stepped over the body of the fallen skinhead and approached Sarah.

"Thank you," Sarah said, unable to keep herself from staring at the strange woman even as she did so.

"You fought back," she said in a creaking voice.

"I beg your pardon?"

"You fought back. So many years, so many centuries I have sought you out, always to have you taken from me before I could get close enough... At first, I didn't care, you see. I revelled in my punishment. I lead my monstrous children to you just to prove to Him how much I laughed at His sentence. But as the slow centuries fell away, I became so tired of this life, so tired... I tried to find you to end it, but always the curse kicked in, always the monsters found you first and cast you beyond my reach. I became so accustomed to watching, helpless... I started to believe I was powerless to ever change things... It consumed me."

"I -- what?" Sarah wanted to take a step back, to put some distance between herself and this strange, rambling woman who could kill a man with her bare hands, but she was transfixed by the deep, blue eyes, by the distance and history within them.

"But this time, you fought back," the woman continued. "I'd forgotten, but you made me remember. And now... and now we are together again."

"Who are you?" Sarah asked, although in her heart she already had a good inkling. What figure had always stood as a critical pivot in her studies -- what figure had, now that she could look back clearly, always drawn her to this line of research?

"Lilith, they call me now," the tramp said, confirming her suspicions.

"I know you," Sarah said. "Somehow, I know I've seen you before."

"Many times, in past lives," Lilith said. "Because of what we share. I was cast out of Eden, millennia ago, for refusing to accept the authority of my husband, and his Lord."

Sarah was startled. Most scholars had thought that particular back-story a recent invention... though, on the other hand, most scholars thought the woman standing before her was entirely fictional as well. And if Lilith was real, then perhaps she had only passed on the true account of her origins in the last few centuries.

"I became a plague on humanity, and mothered many monsters whose malicious impulses of dominance and hate haunt this world still... but only one who was human: my only daughter." Lilith stepped forward, and with the back of her hand caressed Sarah's cheek. "To ensure that His exile held, that I could never return to the afterlife, He tore me asunder. I was riven, my soul split from my body and entwined with hers, trapping it in her mortal shell. When you died, my soul left this world along with yours, until such time that you were reborn. And every time I came close to finding you, my children, who answer to Him as surely as all creatures but myself, would kill you again, stealing you away from me. And without a soul, I was condemned to walk the Earth in perpetuity."

Lilith stared at her levelly.

81

"I am tired of this world, as I told you. I want to shuffle off this mortal coil. I want my soul back."

"Hey, hold on a minute," Sarah said, holding her hands out. "I'm still using this soul."

"The bounty of the spirit is infinite," Lilith said. "It can be shared without ever being lost."

"Like a cold," Sarah said hesitantly.

"Like love," Lilith whispered.

"How...?"

Lilith shushed her, crossed the remaining distance between them, and pressed her lips to Sarah's. Sarah, surprised, did not return the kiss; it didn't feel sensual, anyway, not like something she would share with Olivia, but with an affectionate family member instead. Sarah felt a rush of wind in her throat and mouth, and when Lilith pulled away, her face was transforming. Lines vanished, sagging flesh firmed, grey hair found its colour once more; soon she looked young and powerful, like the priestess Sarah had seen in her first dream.

Or rather, memory.

"Thank you," Lilith said. "Thank you for reminding me of who I am, and for granting me my release. It is long since time I went home and settled some scores." Her lips curled into a smile. "I don't think they'll be happy to see me."

As Sarah watched, Lilith seemed to vibrate, shimmering until she became translucent, and then her entire body launched upwards in a white flame, like a bolt of lightning in reverse, and vanished into the clear night sky.

Sarah watched the heavens for a few minutes, wondering if she would see some further sign of Lilith. The sound of sirens, no doubt coming in response to the fire in the library behind her, finally brought her back to reality. She grabbed her bag and resolved not to be around when the authorities found the body of the skinhead Lilith had killed. As she jogged down the street, she heard a roll and crack of thunder, though there wasn't a cloud in the sky when she looked up.

Sarah smiled to herself. Lilith was home. And there

would be hell to pay.

Maria received her Ph. D. in Theoretical Chemistry from the University of Toronto. She has published four books (in Persian) and over a hundred essays, articles, and interviews in print and online media. Maria has received grants for English literature and residency at The Banff Centre from Ontario Arts Council, City of Ottawa, and Canada Council for the Arts and served on art juries. Currently, Maria is writing a collection of short stories about daily lives of Iranians prior to 1979 revolution in Iran.

http://mariasabaye.blogspot.ca

Sorority of the Defeated
by Maria Sabaye Moghaddam

My earliest memory of Major Adibi's wife coincides with my first sighting of the ocean. Thirty years ago, the day after my fifth birthday, we took a trip to a small town near Bushehr on the coast of the Persian Gulf. At dawn, we arrived at our friend's white, one-story villa with palm trees lining the driveway. As I stepped out of the car, I was greeted by the distant sound of waves and a thin layer of moisture that wrapped itself around me.

A tall, brown-skinned woman with long blonde hair in a green, sleeveless dress greeted my parents at the door.

"I was just going for a swim," she said in a low voice, "Everyone else is sleeping."

"Alone? At this hour?" my mother murmured.

"How is the Major?" my father asked with a yawn, and without waiting for an answer, continued, "I can't keep my eyes open any longer. I am heading for bed. Where is our room?"

Major Adibi's wife pointed to a door at the end of the corridor. She then noticed me hiding behind my mother. She bent down and held out her arms.

"And how is the birthday girl?" she said with a beaming smile.

I let go of my mother's skirt, wondering how the woman knew about my birthday.

"She slept all the way," said my mother. "I had to talk to the doctor all night to keep him from dozing off at the wheel." She yawned and tugged at my arm to move.

I resisted. "I want to see the ocean."

"What's there to see? It's just water," my mother said, in

85

an irritated voice.

"It's not just water," I said and twisting my arm from her grasp, I headed to the car to get my globe, which showed the contours of the ocean.

"Why don't I take her with me? I was going anyway." Major Adibi's wife came to my rescue.

My mother seemed too tired to argue; she gave in and went inside. I followed Major Adibi's wife into the backyard, where white, yellow, and purple petunias ran along two sides of a small, empty pool. As Major Adibi's wife took long strides, her golden pony tail, held high with a long green ribbon, swayed from side to side. The ruffle at the hem of her skirt rose with the breeze, revealing the back of her brown knees, before it gently floated back down. She picked up a large tin pail, a smaller red bucket, and two rusty little shovels to make up a sand castle kit for me.

Taking the sandy side road to the beach, we followed the moist, cool breeze which smelled of brine. The sun was rising in the distant horizon, spreading a thin, sheen carpet upon the surface of the water. It surprised me that, unlike the sketch on my globe, there was no land, no end really. Water covered the earth until it merged with the sky.

At the shore, the waves roared high and splashed salt water that stung our faces, arms, and legs. Rolling up my half-wet skirt, I retreated. Major Adibi's wife didn't seem to mind; stretching out her long brown arms, she ran into the waves. Stepping back, she burst into laughter, shook her head, and then wiped her large eyes with her hands.

"I am going in," she yelled.

I felt a sharp pang at the thought of being on the beach all by myself, but she disappeared before I could say anything. At a distance from the waves, I set up my tools and began digging roads and constructing bridges in the sand. A ship blew its horn in the distance. I looked up. Far out to my left a motorboat rode close to a ship. I watched until both vessels passed out of view, and when I turned back to the sea in front of me, I could not see Major Adibi's wife. I stood up and tried to call her, but no sound came. Suddenly something drew my eyes far out ahead of me. Somewhere in what appeared to be in the middle of the ocean, Major Adibi's wife stood waist deep, her silhouette cutting the rising sun into halves. I lost all fear and ran towards her, fixing my gaze on the silhouette and calling and waving. For a brief moment she disappeared. Then her right arm came out of the water, and then the left, and then the right. She was swimming back towards the shore.

Finally, she rose from the ocean, white surf foaming at her knees. With water dripping from her golden pony tail and her wet dress hugging her curves, she seemed like a creature from a fairytale, a mermaid perhaps. She rolled her green skirt to one side and wrung out the water. Then something in the sand caught her attention. She let go of her skirt and picked up the tin pail. I resumed my play in the sand as she walked around half bent, every now and then picking up something red or cream-coloured and dropping it into the pail.

"I thought you were going to the end of the ocean," I said to her when she finally squatted beside my sand bridge.

She ruffled my hair and smiled.

"What for? The sky is the same color on the other side."

We watched the water spray as the motes flickered, changing colors in the sunshine. The sand was warm and soft, and the air wafting from the bucket smelled heavily of salt and fish. Three red and two cream coloured crabs scuttled at the bottom of the pail. All those claws moving about in different directions made me cringe. I wanted to turn away when I noticed one red crab with a black dot on its back scrape the pail's side. It clung onto the small patches of sand stuck on the steep, metal wall and clambered up the side. The other crabs stayed stuck at the bottom of the pail, as if trying to understand the situation, before they stretched up and grabbed the one climbing. After some pulling and pushing, the red crab fell back into the bucket. Five pairs of claws intertwined and formed the rings of a chain, which held them together, motionless.

My stomach turned when they stopped moving altogether.

"They're dead."

Major Adibi's wife glanced at the crabs and drew me near.

"No. They resigned," she said calmly, as if stating a fact.

"Why did they claw that one down?"

"Why indeed?" she said with sort of a sigh, turning her gaze in the direction of the house. "They'll be worried. We should go back."

Major Adibi, an old friend of my father, and his wife were frequent visitors to our house. Friends both old and new, relatives, and acquaintances, often accompanied by their own group of friends, came to lunch or dinner two or three times a month. Life seemed like an everlasting party to me, unperturbed by the changes in faces, outfits, and names of those who washed up at the shores of my parents' busy social life in the early seventies in Tehran. The guests were entertained in two large rooms leading to the terrace on the second floor. One room was furnished with beautiful carpets and sofas and armchairs, and the other with an exquisite dining table, which could seat twelve people.

Most of our visitors, Major Adibi for example, left their children at home so they could stay late and enjoy themselves. For that reason, these parties did not appeal to me until I was in third grade, when I began losing friends throughout the school year for seemingly no reason at all. I was used to being popular, having a best friend, a close circle of five or six friends, and many acquaintances. At some point, I noticed my friends gradually stopped inviting me to their birthday parties or after school activities. I was in denial at first. Confusion ensued, followed by ill-concealed embarrassment and hurt when they avoided me at the games we had always played during our breaks. I didn't understand what was happening, and I was too proud to ask. I spent hours reviewing the events prior to the onslaught of this cold front, but except for a prize for my composition on my goal of becoming an astronaut it had been quite an uneventful year. When my mother inquired why I hadn't brought her the registration paper for the summer camp, I saved face by saying that it was cancelled due to an outburst of chicken pox. By the time my birthday came in the spring, I swallowed most of my pain and convinced myself that I didn't need a bunch of kids anyway.

And so, my attention turned to what was left – adults. I not only began to take a genuine interest in their parties, but actively engaged in them.

My mother and I began preparing for such gatherings a few days in advance. Zari, an old maid, who shared her time between our household and Aunt Mitra's, was recruited for a thorough cleaning: the wide stone staircase and its metal railing, the floors, the intricately designed Persian carpets, and the huge glass chandeliers. My mother took charge of cooking while the lighter jobs, like dusting the seventy-five little figurines in the china cabinet, were left to me.

After the cleaning, the new tablecloth, the good dishes, and the imported chocolates came out of their hideouts. My mother's watchful eyes ensured they took their rightful places. She was meticulous about the menu: there had to be a soup, a salad (fresh vegetables in summer and cooked beans and potatoes in winter), a basket of fresh herbs, one or two side dishes, one meat and one chicken stew. My mother's continuous offering kept the guests busy emptying one plate after another, and there was always too much food even after guests had their second or third helpings.

However, every time Major Adibi and his wife came, my mother hesitated before bringing out the expensive, hand-embroidered tablecloth. As for the menu, she wouldn't go to the trouble of preparing many of her specialties. Normally, she drained the rice after boiling it, and then spread a mixture of yogurt, rice, saffron, and butter in the bottom of the pot before topping it with rice. The whole dish was steam cooked for an exact length of time -- known to her through experience -- so that the crust in the bottom perfected to a golden, crunchy tah dig. When Major Adibi's family came to visit, my mother settled for the easiest and simplest choices: a plain crust of bread browned at the bottom of the rice pan in a thin layer of oil, and Danish pastries from the bakery instead of the expensive, imported chocolates.

Major Adibi's wife didn't seem to notice or care about what or how she was served; she tossed off compliments wholeheartedly and helped herself to seconds, frequently half rising from her chair as she reached for something across the table while her sleeve picked up flakes of rice or drops of juice from the food on the way. I could hear the voice in my mother's head as her anxious eyes traced the colored trail, "what is best for removing oil and tomato stains?"

Nobody could say Major Adibi's wife was good looking or chic. She had a large, hooked nose and dyed blond hair that clashed with her dark skin and eyebrows. In winter, she would sometimes wear a striped, nylon blouse with a checkered wool skirt and a large belt with decorative metal petals around its eyelets.

"She has no sense of pattern," Aunt Mitra, my mother's younger sister, would say, "And that gruesome belt!"

Or Major Adibi's wife would wear tight jeans with a tucked in soft, flared, floral shirt; this would create a stir.

"A married woman, a married woman with children, showing her –", my mother's eyes flicked from Aunt Mitra to me, then back to stop her from saying ass in front of me.

I wanted to defend Major Adibi's wife, but I didn't know how. Just like Aunt Mitra, I thought, to turn everyone's clothing into a story of disgrace. I would never say this out loud, of course. Just as I would never say that I didn't like Aunt Mitra's constant visits to our home. After she returned from England, I expected her -- we all did -- to go back to my grandmother's house in Sanandaj. But she stayed with us for eight months, and then married a local diplomat, who traveled all the time. She didn't like being alone, she said, and so she spent most of her time at our house, where her hours were filled by visits to the hairdresser, three times a week for color, wax, thread and what not, and a few high end boutiques, open to special customers only by appointment. I never saw a book in her hand, and she openly expressed disdain, even contempt, for everything I admired -- books, poetry, stories. I would attempt retaliation by finding some fault with her: if she pulled her hair back very tightly, her forehead would seem too high; though her nose was small and slender, one nostril was slightly larger than the other (you had to peer very carefully to notice); and sometimes, her unblemished skin would be stained by a stubborn pimple under her right eye. Despite these flaws, most of which were discovered by me and with great concentration and effort, she looked stunning in her tailored dresses and suits, which hugged her tall, sensuous figure. She was lively, full of energy and confidence. The only times I had seen her subdued and withdrawn were after she returned from her house. Every other month, her husband spent a week or two at home between his travels, and Aunt Mitra joined him. There was something about these visits that I couldn't understand until years later: the long-sleeve, loose dresses with high necklines she wore or the absent-minded, dazed expression that lingered on her face for a while after her husband had left.

It wasn't just Aunt Mitra's dislike of books that bothered me, but also her constant criticism of my mother for letting me get too close to 'that woman', meaning Major Adibi's wife. One afternoon my mother and I were flipping through magazines in the kitchen, looking at pictures to choose a pattern for my new dress. I pointed to a picture of a dark woman wearing a floral dress with a large belt.

"I like this one."

Aunt Mitra glanced at the photo, ran her long fingers through her black hair.

"What do you expect?" she said, turning to my mother.

I didn't understand for a moment.

"What next? You are going to let her dye her hair yellow?"

She continued, with a fake expression of amusement on her face.

"I like... Major Adibi's wife." It suddenly occurred to me that I never knew her name, first or last, or any other woman for that matter, except for Aunt Mitra and my mother. And then to balk Aunt Mitra, I said something else.

"She has many remarkable qualities."

At this, a spiteful grin dawned on Aunt Mitra's face.

"Oh, really? Name one?"

She knew very well, just as I did, that I wasn't able to name any such qualities. Except in writing, I often failed to articulate or explain what I sensed about the attitudes and actions of those around me. Perhaps it was also a matter of comprehension. I sensed things about Major Adibi's wife: her air of confidence that obliged the company, regardless of age or gender, to acknowledge her presence. Unlike the other married women, she called her husband by his first name and not his title. Nor did she huddle with the other women in the kitchen to talk about aching backs, sleepless babies, or the latest fashion trends. She seemed to prefer the company of men, something the other women found 'unnatural'.

After dinner at our parties, my father and the other men often rested in the armchairs and sofas, drank vodka, and discussed such issues as the price of oil and the balance of power in the Middle East. The women often gossiped at the kitchen table or in the hall, except when Major Adibi's wife was around, when they reluctantly joined the men. My mother's views on everything from famine in Africa to the war in the Middle East was that "it's the Brits' doing" -- in line with the national distrust of the British, responsible for anything that went wrong anywhere. The other women didn't feel a need to express or have an opinion and seemed overly content, almost proud of their ignorance. Aunt Mitra had lived in the UK for a year and her husband, the diplomat, spent most of his time overseas. But every time I asked her where her new pair of shoes or a bag or a dress came from, she would shrug and say, "Some shop, I guess."

Major Adibi's wife didn't have political views so far away from those of the rest of the women, but she read the papers, knew her geography, and recounted specific stories about heads of states or their families. One evening, when we were all in the living room, she brought up a true story of the wife of a president who owned five thousand pairs of shoes. This prompted a lively conversation among the usually passive women. "Does she have matching handbags and gloves in the same color or can she choose different shades?" The women divided in two camps which vehemently vied for one option over the other. Any debate on fashion was settled by Aunt Mitra, the expert, and this was no exception. She left the living room for a few moments and returned with the latest issue of a women's magazine, her and my mom's favorite. She tossed it on the table, took her seat, and flipped to the page with three photos of the president's wife in one of her official visits to Russia wearing handbags and shoes in different shades of beige, purple, and blue. The men sat in silence, drinking and watching the women with a tender, amused look in their eyes.

Major Adibi's wife picked up the magazine and turned to the cover, which showed a photo of a woman with a round face and a large pair of glasses, framed by a black chador.

"At least she doesn't have to worry about matching colors," she said in a bitter tone and put the magazine back on the table.

We all knew the woman on the cover. After thirteen years of marriage, Fatemeh had shot her husband thirteen times in the fall of 1972. The prosecutor had asked for maximum punishment, a sentence which was deemed unjust by the few women's associations and societies which defended women's rights.

"I hope she gets what she deserves," Aunt Mitra said, scrutinizing her fingernails.

"Deserves? She was beaten regularly by her husband, a police officer. Once she complained to her husband's superior, and she ended up with two broken ribs," Major Adibi's wife said.

"The police are not allowed to interfere in family affairs," a guest, who happened to be a lawyer, attested, sorting out the legal issues. Apparently, the law considered men beating their wives or children a private matter.

"Now, we can't have women running around murdering their husbands, can we?" my father said with such conviction that, at first, I agreed with him. Then it occurred to me that I had never heard him question men killing their wives, sisters or daughters, a fairly regular subject on the news.

"What about the children?" My mother interjected. "How could they bear the shame of being orphans with a killer as their mother?"

"A murderer is a murderer," Aunt Mitra said and pushed the magazine away contemptuously.

"He gave her syphilis, which the doctor wouldn't treat without the bastard's permission. He deserved every bullet," Major Adibi's wife said.

I noticed how my mother winced twice at the mention of the words syphilis and bastard. Yet, in the heat of the moment, I lost control and uttered, "One bullet for each year. That seems fair!"

The room fell silent. My father rose from his chair.

Major Adibi's wife, grasping the gravity of the moment, continued where I left off.

"Yes, indeed. Let that be a warning to all wicked men." She winked at me from across the room.

My father sat down, his gaze fixed on me. My mother's eyes turned to slits as she opened her mouth, but she swallowed her words. Ordinarily, my father would have yelled or slapped me to put me in my place, and my mother would have said, in a disgusted tone, that she didn't like to hear her child say such things. This I detested as much as the slap. It wasn't the reference to me as a child that bothered me most; I was soon to be thirteen. It was her constant demands of conformity to her likes and dislikes that made me resentful. That night, however, my father averted his eyes, and my mother cast a glance of disapproval in my direction. unt Mitra pretended to be busy with her nails. I felt an immense relief, almost like a triumph. Major Adibi's wife had put everyone in a corner, where they couldn't touch me.

For a while, the only sound was the ice cubes hitting the glass as Major Adibi's wife swished her drink. She goes far, far too far this time, I could imagine each of them thinking. But oblivious to everyone, she took one sip after another under the glare of her husband.

"What about dinner?" My father broke the silence. My mother and Aunt Mitra rose at the same time.

"Shouldn't you give them a hand?" My father's tone assured me his question was an order. I was happy to leave, probably everyone would have been.

"What can I do to help?" I said, once I was in the kitchen.

My mother was in such desperate need of extra hands to do the finishing touches on the dishes that she had no time, or interest it seemed, to scold me.

After dinner, Major Adibi's wife turned to my mother.

"You have done enough. We will take it from here."

She swiveled her neck in my direction, and I followed her into the kitchen. She washed the dishes, I dried them. She had been unusually quiet the rest of the evening. Half way through the dishes, she dropped everything into the basin, filled a glass half with vodka, half with ice, sat down at the table, and lit a cigarette. I stopped drying and sat across from her.

"My mother married me off before I finished high school," she said, as if speaking to herself, her gaze fixed on her glass on a plate full of orange peel and seeds on the table. "I guess she had to. One less mouth to feed."

She took a deep puff on her cigarette. "My sisters envied me. They didn't know what it was like at the husband's house." She raised the glass to her lips, muttering what I thought were curses directed at Major Adibi, before telling me about her finishing high school at his house, studying mainly at night after everyone was asleep. "When I showed my mother the diploma, she sneered."

"'Not thick enough to wipe off your baby's bottom. He wants a son, not a wife with a piece of paper, remember?'"

"Your sisters must have been happy for you."

"Happy!" She tapped her cigarette into an orange peel on the plate. "They never got over my marrying an army officer. Two of them settled for cab drivers, one for a peddler."

Up to that point, I had had no idea that Major Adibi's wife came from such a poor family. Was her poverty the reason for my mother's dislike of her? Words of apology kept forming in my head, in my mouth, but none came out. My throat knotted.

Major Adibi's wife reached for her handbag on the counter. She rummaged through it, pulling out a folded newspaper. There was a glitter in her eyes as she held it out.

"Guess what? Here it is: my name! Mine! Accepted in the university--"

"Really?" I couldn't imagine "old" people -- anyone above twenty seemed old to me -- attending university. I spread the newspaper on the table and smoothed out the creases. The wobbly, red circle around her name, Fatemeh Mehrabi (so she did have a name of her own), made it easy to find. I imagined her anxious eyes roaming over the list of hundreds of names on the paper, her disbelief and ecstasy at finding her own, jumping up, searching for a pen, a red one to be sure (it had to stand out), then worrying that it might be a namesake, dropping the pen, running her finger across the row to the last column to check the ID number, picking up the pen again, and drawing a circle with a shaky hand.

Her voice brought me back to the kitchen. "'You won't make a cuckold of me. I won't have my wife sitting beside men,' he says. And my mother applauds him."

I was about to declare my condemnation of her mother

and husband when Aunt Mitra barged in, her eyes roving. I pretended to be absorbed in the paper, which caught her attention. She came close and bent over it for a few moments before she suddenly straightened herself up.

"It's her name," I pointed to the red circle -- fully aware that she must have spotted it and guessed whose name it was.

"Oh," Aunt Mitra said as if she had just remembered what she wanted. She rushed towards the dish rack beside the sink, picked up a plate, and left.

After the party was over, I listened to Aunt Mitra and my mother in the kitchen, talking with quiet, anxious voices. I knew from experience that the best concealment was to sit quietly in a corner.

"What was that all about?" Aunt Mitra smirked. "That woman! Going to university at her age?" She sounded as if she had been deeply insulted – by that woman's intention of pursuing higher education or her acceptance to university, I couldn't tell, but it wasn't her age because Major Adibi's wife was about the same age as Aunt Mitra, who never thought she would be too old for anything.

My mother tilted her head to one side, looking pensive.

"Major Adibi can be a handful, but she must have known that right from the start."

"And what exactly is wrong with Major Adibi?" Aunt Mitra asked.

"Well, you know, he is not quite the ideal husband."

"Women wouldn't leave him alone, for sure. She should be grateful he hasn't taken a second wife."

"If he did, it would be the third," my mother said.

"You knew all along? Who is she?" Aunt Mitra leaned forward, bobbing her head, and tapping her fingers on the table. My mother didn't seem to share her amusement.

"He was very young when he first married, but the woman couldn't bring him a son. His family was desperate.

He is their only son. So he married her. You know what they say, younger woman, older man have better chance of having a son."

Aunt Mitra paused to disentangle a few strands of hair from the grip of her multiple-tiered necklace.

"So what? He pays for that ridiculous colour she puts in her hair, doesn't he? The shoes, the clothes... did you see her new broach? All that for a peddler's daughter."

"Don't say that. The poor are human too." My mother declared this with the conviction of a champion of altruism. One could say she was if compared to Aunt Mitra. She often gave food to the poor coming to our door but never let them in. Passers-by watched as they buried their faces in the bowl and ate the food in the street.

Aunt Mitra sat bolt upright and raised her eyebrows. "We all have to make sacrifices. I gave up school to look after Mother."

"Oh, dear, not that again. You never had any interest in school."

"Not true. I came back for the sake of Mother."

"You never set foot in Sanandaj in fifteen years. How did you intend to take care of her from here?"

"What happened to your career?" Aunt Mitra countered.

My mother looked down - her voice sinking into a whisper.

"What could I do? I was expecting. My having a career wasn't meant to be."

"I'm sorry. You are right. We can't change what is meant to be."

I slipped away from the kitchen, climbed into my bed, and pulled the blanket over my face. Aunt Mitra's words -- what is meant to be -- echoed in my head as I stared into the darkness, grinding my teeth.

The Adibis' visits came to a halt after that night. It was

not unusual for people to appear and disappear at the scene of my parents' lunches and dinners. Old friends or relatives, separated from my parents by job transfers or family obligations, would show up at our door unexpectedly, and we welcomed them most warmly. They would join others in our parties, enjoying the hospitality until the next transfer or family problem came up. What made the Adibis' absence different was that there was no mention of such excuses; in fact there was no mention of them at all. It might have been due to two major events that happened that week: my grandparents arrived from Sanandaj, and I won a prize in composition from the school board. Perhaps the issue was lost in the ensuing enthusiasm. No one else seemed to notice, or acknowledge, that the Adibis visits to our house had come to an end. Our life went on as if they had never existed.

It would be five years before I'd see Major Adibi's wife again. This time, it was at their new house to celebrate her husband's promotion to colonel. The invitation led to a row as my mother refused to attend. But my father made it clear that he wouldn't miss celebrating his old friend's success and that there was no way he would go alone. My mother turned to me with pleading eyes.

"Well, don't count on me," I said to my mother.

I had just started university. Busy with my schoolwork, my friends, and my new student life, I couldn't spare a moment.

"She phoned and asked specifically for you," my mother responded.

Her asking for me affected me. It is only a few hours anyway, I thought, and decided to go along.

We drove to the outskirts of Tehran, into a suburb-to-be, one of the new developments northwest of the city with promises of future increased value. People who could not afford a large, elaborate house in an established neighborhood in Tehran often moved out to such areas where the land was cheap. We got lost twice because most of the streets did not yet have lights or proper signs. Aunt Mitra rolled up the window as we traveled along the gravel road leading to their house. At first, it seemed that the house was suspended in air: the top floor, glittering with light, hovered over the darkness below. My father turned on the high beam, illuminating the bricks on the half walls that skirted the house.

Major Adibi greeted us at the door. We followed him into a large, multi-level hall with large chandeliers hanging from the high ceiling. Huge paintings of landscapes, animals -- probably prints - mirrors, and decorative carpets hung from walls. Well over twenty guests -- I didn't recognize anyone except for the lawyer with the goatee -- were spread about on a set of huge, brown furniture in the living room. The large windows were covered with two sets of drapes. The bottom layer was a thick beige fabric, the top one a ruffled, thin brown lace, a long layer of which was also spread on the dining room table. Two middle-aged women in blue uniforms were placing large serving dishes on the dinner table. We were unfashionably late.

"I told him you were lost," Major Adibi's wife said with a smile. "Everyone is starving!"

She was wearing a navy chiffon blouse tucked into a long pleated, floral skirt with high heels. Her hair was now dark brown with grey roots showing at her temples. Her mouth turned down permanently at the corners. She looked rather subdued, perhaps owing to the pressure of having had two more children since I last saw her. We were immediately led to the table where five or six whole roasted chickens, large silver trays full of rice, salad, and two meat stews were laid.

Throughout the dinner, I noticed my mother and Aunt Mitra made unprecedented, sincere attempts at having a conversation with Major Adibi's wife from across the table.

I heard my mother congratulating her on having "two gems" (her two sons). When Major Adibi's wife pointed to her grey roots, Aunt Mitra told her that she had just found this little hairdresser who did long-lasting marvels with just that sort of thing. I never dreamed Aunt Mitra would share her hairdresser, dressmaker, or in fact anything to do with her appearance, with anybody, let alone with Major Adibi's wife, but there she was rummaging through her handbag looking for a piece of paper to write a name and a phone number down. Then came my mother's invitation for a get together at our place, just like old times, my mother said, as if remembering those 'old times' fondly. The source of this sudden generosity of spirit baffled me for a moment. Their obliging attitude went beyond common courtesy -- something they never bothered with five years ago -- and resembled a ceremonious gesture of acceptance or initiation. They were kind and forgiving toward Major Adibi's wife, whose reaction was varied. At times she reciprocated their enthusiasm as if she welcomed this new interest on their part. Other times she nodded and gently withdrew from them with a faint smile on her lips.

It was after dinner that she began drinking and started to resemble her old self. She became the centre of attention, but this time, there was no mention of politics. She told one bad joke after another, laughed at her own jokes, and called to the servers to refresh everyone's drinks though it was mostly hers that needed refilling.

Bored and embarrassed -- why was I ever drawn to her? -- I looked at my watch (again) and headed toward the terrace. In the quiet of the night, I settled into one of the chairs. The voices inside drifted out as I stared at the glittering sky, darkened here and there by a few clouds. The clouds shifted about, revealing a half-moon and a long array of stars, large and small, white and yellow, glowing in clusters. Just like when

I was a child, I imagined myself an astronaut, weightless and free, hopping about from one planet to the next. My thoughts drifted to that day in third grade, when I shared my dream of becoming an astronaut. "You think you are different, but you're not," my best friend had said in a tone that held both disappointment and hurt. When did that dream change to becoming an earthbound writer? "Writers and poets, they all starve," my father had always said.

"Look what I have here!"

Major Adibi's wife interrupted my thoughts. She was standing in the door way with a cigarette in one hand, a half-filled glass in the other, holding something under the crook of her arm. She dropped a photo album on my lap and slumped onto a cushioned bench across from me. I opened the book and in the dim light of the terrace peered at the black and white pictures of Major Adibi's parents, followed by his photos in army uniform and three wedding pictures. There were no photos of the parents of Major Adibi's wife. In all three snapshots, Major Adibi and his wife stood behind a wedding cake decorated with artificial roses and pearls with Major Adibi's parents on one side and four giggling girls in sleeveless dresses on the other while four or five children played under the table.

Then there were a few colour ones from that first trip to the ocean. One, taken on the day we'd gone to the beach together. The families stood in a row with their shared white villa in the background. Major Adibi's wife was in the centre of the photo, sunlight reflected off the tin crab pail at her foot. Leaning to the left with one hand on her waist, she held forth a crab by its claws in a gesture of comic defiance. The men had spread about her with amusement on their faces. Aunt Mitra had an expression bordering on disgust, and my mother had forced out a smile that barely hid her hostility. Only half of my profile was in the picture, one eye, tip of my nose, and less than half a gaping mouth, beaming from the far right corner.

Once again my thoughts drifted back to that day in third

grade. The girls' averted faces, their pouts, and their muted anger reminded me of something that had eluded my grasp.

Major Adibi's wife tapped on my shoulder. "Where did you disappear to?"

What did she mean? Now? Or then? Shouldn't I have asked that question? Had I ever asked about her? I couldn't remember. Perhaps I did, and my mother put me off with some vague reply. Then again, perhaps I didn't. I told myself that I was too young to grasp the isolation and loneliness, hers and mine, amidst the solidarity of those, not so unwillingly, defeated. This should have convinced me since I had always thought I was different, different from my mother, my aunt, and all those other women I held in contempt, but it didn't.

"I'm sorry," I said in a rush.

She rose from the bench, sat in a chair closer to me, and together we stared at the sky.

Kate is currently finishing her MA in Disability Studies in Winnipeg where her research interests include representations of disability in both fiction and nonfiction (with a personal interest in how this plays out in science fiction and fantasy). Her writing has appeared in Prairie Fire, As it Ought to Be, geez magazine, and Wordgathering. In the summer of 2014 she was the inaugural Writer in Residence at the Manitoba Writers' Guild where she blogged at mylittlecrippledheart.wordpress.com. The curly-haired guy in her story might very well be her dream lover.

Preventative Measures
by Kate Grisim

Fiona never knew her body could be a commodity. She had never thought of it that way, except as perhaps a game the Gods, (or Robots), had made up as a cruel joke.

Until she was, at the risk of sounding dramatic, accosted last Tuesday.

She was on her way to lunch, hobbling as fast as her technologically manufactured right leg could take her. She was thinking about the class she had just come out of, Technologies of the Past, and how glad she was to have skipped that time suck (what the hell was a floppy disk? How did anyone think that was useful technology?) when she almost fell on top of two Humans with their tongues down each other's throats. They were rolling back and forth, attached to each other as if each new angle would give them a different taste of what they were looking for. A string or a button from their clothes snagged on a wire in her calf responsible for one of her toes, and she nearly fell on top of the lusty twosome. She managed to straighten herself up before they even registered what happened. They detached long enough for the Male one to huff, "Watch it, Accustom."

They went back to sucking face as if she were merely disposable, really nothing to pay attention to or be concerned about. In doing so they missed her "don't-worry-I'm-invincible" look, which wasn't all that convincing anyway.

She was taking a short cut through the only two bushes left in the quad --vegetation, it was decided twenty years ago, was no longer necessary -- when she felt a Human hand on her hip.

At first she thought it might be one of the Humans in heat coming to say sorry. She stopped in her twisted tracks, but found that it wasn't a Human. It was a Collector; it said so on his badge. She hadn't been touched so intimately for years, so that she felt accosted seemed appropriate.

The Collector must have looked kind of nice when he wasn't accosting young women on campus grounds, Fiona imagined. He wore a loose jacket that hung on his frame like a wire coat hanger was still stuck in it. His badge was displayed proudly over his heart with the "r" written backwards. A dusty top hat sat atop his head at a jaunty angle as a curious addition to his overall appearance. He looked pathetic and tired, the bags under his eyes bruised like overripe fruit. Fiona didn't know whether to hug him or run away.

He talked as if he had done this many times, but the words streaming out of his mouth were so confusing Fiona felt as though she was a stranger on another planet.

Well, and she wasn't really listening.

"...so they sent me to ask you to consider their offer to take you in. I'm sorry if I scared you. I try to make it a point not to scare people. Life's scary enough, in my humble opinion."

"Well, maybe you should work on that." Fiona took a step back. "Are you actually saying someone wants to adopt me?"

"Adopt' is the antiquated term, but essentially that's correct."

"This a joke, right?"

"I'd never joke about something as serious as Collecting."

"And explain why they would want me again?"

"For your parts, of course."

"My parts?"

"Please forgive me, there are so many new terms, and I'm due for an update soon." He unfolded a creased piece of paper from his pocket. "Your custom-made parts, I mean."

"You mean my leg? Why would anyone want my leg?"

"Technically -- and I'm sorry if no one told you this, my dear -- they're the property of --"

She waved his comment away as if he were a pesky fly. "But I'm, um, using it currently."

"Oh, yes, there's no question of that. No, not at all." He actually chuckled. For all the gravity his words contained, he sure brought a cheerful disposition to his work. "No, this couple would like you to become their Collected for the prestige it would bring them."

"I'm going to bring someone prestige? How the fuck would I do that? What exactly am I worth?" Her mind was reeling. "And, um, I've already got parents. Have you checked with them first?"

"They were made quite aware this might happen one day."

"Well I sure as hell wasn't."

"It's all in the contract."

"This was arranged? In writing?"

"I can see I've caught you unaware. I apologize, but this is not really in my job description."

"Wait a minute: you're telling me my parents were aware I might be taken from them, someone else wants me now, and it's all because of this?"

"Erm. Precisely," the Collector answered sheepishly.

Her right leg was a mesh of wire, hardware, and chrome. She had lived with it for so long she didn't know where she actually ended and her artificial limb began. She had been born with a leg -- a real one -- she knew that. The Doctor had told her parents it wouldn't develop right, so at three months old she had surgery to get a new one fused to her bones; Preventative Measures was the new-fangled term. Her Mother often used the phrase ironically, as if it should have quotes around it. Fiona had been one of the first hundred to have a successful surgery in North America. She was featured in an anatomy textbook, her three-month-old leg diagrammed and labelled accordingly. She was somewhat famous in the Advanced Kinesiology department.

Fiona sensed that her Mother didn't quite believe in the field as radically as others did, or at least in what was at the root of the gesture to help. But she didn't really have any other choice.

The sad reality was that Fiona had come out lucky, if anything. She knew a lot of people younger than her who had more chrome in their bodies than actual human tissue. The new ad campaigns were trying to sell the products the medical field offered as badges of honour. More and more people were becoming Accustomed, like it wasn't a big deal at all.

But she never thought she'd be wanted for her legs. Or one of them, anyway. She had never felt special. Only... tampered with.

Her heart liked the feeling of someone wanting her; her head wondered why. She had grown up ignoring that part of her, though, and proceeded to do so now. The important thing was that she was wanted, whatever the reason.

No one had wanted to be an Accustom earlier on in the century when they were still referred to as Human, even though everyone had their own secret name for an Accustom anyway. What had changed was that someone, though it was a heated debate exactly who--main contesters were the banks and the social media networkers, obviously -- had figured out that if they were treated like they were wanted, things would be better for everyone in the long run. Also, they were still misunderstood enough to evoke pity for both themselves and their caregivers. Pity had turned into a kind of currency. No one really wanted to have it, but if you chose it for yourself, you were basically worshipped.

Preventative Measures was, indeed, a field of burgeoning medical science that was so hot it might implode. Prosthetic limbs weren't the only form of technology sought, either. Not only was every actual and imagined limb available, but there were even rumours that prosthetic brains and personalities (set to default, of course, and customized according to the buyer's wishes) were about to be patented. Virtually no one could keep up with the money the field consumed at a rapid pace, as if blimps full of hundred dollar bills had appeared in the sky nearly twenty years ago (which was, more often than not, considered ancient history) and it had been raining money consistently ever since. As long as it continued to be profitable, the question of unsound ethics was a moot point.

And ever since the population of Accustoms in the prolific West had more than doubled since Fiona's childhood, everyone wanted to get their hands on one. Humans just couldn't get enough authenticity. It took no time at all until the first custom-made parts were sold on the black market either by force or when the Accustom had no use for them anymore. With this came the revelation that the next-of-kin of an Accustom was a self-made millionaire waiting to happen, their loved one's leftovers becoming the next deal of the day in back channels on eBay and onepartfitsall.com. More often than not, though, the technology was so advanced that previous models soon became obsolete and usually ended up in some remote part of the world in a heap of garbage.

Fiona was used to being a Patient, or as used as one could get to being a Patient after spending weeks at a time in the Hospital as a child. She never could get over how exposed she was always made to feel. Case in point: all that separated her parts now from the disinfectant-tinged air was a dingy swath of blue paper. She could never shake the feeling that others thought her parts were all she added up to.

What made it worse was that her leg had never been hers, not really -- the Collector, whose name turned out to be Danny, had been nice enough to peruse the contract with her on the way over -- but now that someone else wanted it, she felt she didn't want to give it up. She would take her lilting gait, clumsy and zombie-ish though it may be. She would take the way Humans gaped at her still, as though walking was made to be done only one way. She would even take the embarrassment of having to find an electrical outlet when she required a zap of manufactured energy and strength.

She just wanted to be the sole proprietor of her temperamental yet biologically sound limb, so that it was hers and no one else's. Was that really so much to ask?

She felt oddly deflated after the initial high of being wanted had worn off. Now she was just melancholy; melancholy and antiseptic. She had been swabbed and sterilized so well she felt like one of those deceased pets grief-stricken owners got stuffed with cotton and a rudimentary computer system.

Apparently this once-over was part of the deal. A clean Accustom was the only acceptable kind in the eyes of the law. The Doctor had been nice enough, avoiding eye contact when he was examining her hooha. Thankfully that was all well and good and working properly. She half expected a swab to be swiped and placed on her file, but fortunately that uncomfortable moment never came. She was relieved, to say the least. Of all her "issues," she was glad that wasn't one of them.

Every once in a while, she forgot that a part of her body could think on its own.

There was a soft, staccato knock and the Computer Programmer came in with his eyes closed and his hands raised, as if he was caught in a bank robbery. "Are you decent?"

"That's still to be determined."

His eyes opened one at a time, reminding Fiona of the antique dolls her Mother had as a child. Their vivid descriptions had given Fiona nightmares. "You look pretty decent to me." His eyebrows wriggled as if they were chasing each other.

Computer Programmers, once sought after for their ingenuity, were now a dime a dozen. But a good Programmer could still change the world, and they all knew it. Fiona's apartment block was full of them, staying up at all hours of the night glued to their software of choice and their ears stuffed with obscure early-2010 pop music. Her neighbours across the hall went out for ramen at three in the morning, carrying their leftover containers home in a walk of shame as Fiona left for school. When she had tried to make conversation with them to be nice, all they wanted to talk about was either programming or virtual sex.

Despite that, he was rather cute. He had curly hair and mismatched socks and a penchant for twitching. She was tied into a blue sheet. "I feel like a lab experiment."

"You don't look like one."

His loyalty was endearing, but annoying. "You can stop the flattery. I know what other people think I'm worth."

"Do you really?"

"Just do what you came here to do. I can handle it."

"Handle what?"

She gestured to the room around her as if that explained everything. "The next step. Becoming a Collected. I'm a big girl."

He sidled over and started examining her leg. "A person isn't the sum of their parts, you know." He spoke to her artificial shin.

She snorted. "Whoa, whoa, Philosopher King, reel it in. Did you come up with that yourself?"

He smirked shyly. "It was the quote of the day on Twitter."

"At least you come by it honestly. But I don't need to be saved." Her voice wavered slightly. The blue sheet had sweat stains on it from her hands.

"I'm just a Computer Programmer. And you look like you can take care of yourself." He looked her up and down, his Adam's apple bobbing. "Things look good here. I just need to disengage your leg to get a look at the internal wiring."

"Will it hurt?"

"I thought you were a big girl." Blood rushed to his cheeks as he placed a hand tentatively on the place where the bone was fused, right below her kneecap. He shivered. "I never get used to how cold these parts are."

"You get used to it. Eventually, you don't even feel

anything."

He disconnected a wire that made her leg go numb. It was wonderful, as if the weight that had kept her from floating away had been released.

He looked up at Fiona, and she winked. "What's your name?"

Mr. and Mrs. File 333Z were nice people, but they were far from perfect.

When they were married thirty years ago, they both assumed they would start a family right away. That was just how things worked back then. Needless to say, they were caught by surprise when they didn't. Both of them grew a bit colder towards the other, not knowing any other options were available.

They persevered-- a much-admired quality of Humans -- and stayed together out of habit more than anything else. Sex became a duty; passionless, militant, hopeless. They kept doing it just in case a miracle happened.

There was no talk of old-time adoption. Mrs. File 333Z was particularly opposed.

When the field of Preventative Measures boomed, Mr. File 333Z signed them up right away. This is what they had been waiting for all along: an opportunity to seem utterly selfless yet still obtain some kind of compensation for their time.

Then they waited. A Collector found Fiona two years to the day after their file was opened. She was perfect, just what they were looking for. Mrs. File 333Z had wonderful daydreams about bringing Fiona along with her during Saturday errands, like a lap dog.

The day finally came. Their house was vacuumed within an inch of its life.

All they found was a leg on the doorstep. A leg and a note saying, "It's all yours. Knock yourselves out."

Mrs. File 333Z fainted.

Fiona caught the bus out of the city at a back door of the Hospital. She had been told by someone across the hall that busses were coming all the time, shuttling Patients to outside the city where no one wanted to go anyway -- no one except the Accustoms. It was as if they just needed some time out from being wanted. They lived in shacks made of recyclables, she was told, and were much happier.

She still wasn't sure if she had made the right decision. If she became a Collected, she would get everything she ever needed. Everyone would know she was a Collected, and Humans' stares would slide down her back like water. She would be revered and would want for nothing.

That's never what she wanted, though. She had always preferred to blend in.

At the last stop she looked for the mop of curls she couldn't wait to twirl her fingers into. Maybe he wouldn't be there. Maybe it had all been an act. He hadn't seemed that cruel.

She got off the bus, unsteady on one leg and the crutch she had taken from a janitor's closet. Going down stairs was horrendous.

She didn't make it to the ground before she was lifted off her feet. Foot.

He kissed her on the mouth before setting her down. He would need some lessons in one-leggedness, and steadying her. She had no bags.

"So, tell me about virtual sex. Any fun?"

Uzoma Ogbonna is a writer and painter at heart. She holds an honours bachelor of arts degree in English literature and a law degree. She expresses herself in between words and paints. Her works include poetry and short stories published in various literary journals such as The Cave Hill Literary Journal, UC Review: University of Toronto, Nuit Blanche Anthology: Poems for Late Nights and St. Michael's College Magazine.

Poems
by Uzoma Ogbonna

She

She picks the hair off her nipple.
"You have to look the part you know"
-Smiles and bats her lashes.
"You don't know how much work goes into just being..."
Her breasts large and full of milk.
But what is that?!
And she laughs.
This must be the way it feels to be a woman.

Outerbody

When we touched
You felt like mine
hands memorizing your curves
knowing you like myself
I did not know
You
Could feel this way
leaving with that part of me that colonizes

We were only shells of our selves
Our offering self
a raging sea
beyond the grasping
We became beyond the grasping
my great sacrifice now A nothing
An outerbody which you held
long into the blurred line of feeling.

Afterwards
I looked in-ward
and saw you slip like water through my hands
Aching, I offered my outerbody to a being
and looked at you
knowing that I was
a sea beyond my grasping.

Brianna Ferguson earned her Bachelor of Arts degree with a double major in Creative Writing and English from the University of British Columbia in 2016. Her fiction has appeared in Polychrome Ink Literary Magazine, Class Magazine, Effervescent Magazine, and UK based magazine Femmeuary. Her inspirations are Virginia Woolf, Charles Bukowski, and Miranda July. She lives in Kelowna, B.C.

Character-Human
by Brianna Ferguson

Character-human sits alone on a bench beside a river. In the water there is a barge carrying a large, metal storage bin. Two burly men are heaving shovels-full of robotic arms and legs into the bin. They are wearing pin-stripe pants and hats. They don't seem to notice the robot sitting slouched on the bench. Their conversation is on the women they will be entertaining later when the work is done.

Character-human SF-Class cannot move, as the piston in their left leg blew when they sat down. When they were still in the employ of the Callaghan family, they would have dealt immediately with such an issue to avoid any inconvenience in their masters' lives. Now, though, there is no need. They have been dismissed and it is no longer necessary to remain in peak operating condition.

The sun is beginning to set behind the mountains across the river and it glints dully on Character-human's bronze body, disappearing in patches where the dust and the grease have become too built-up to allow the metal to shine through. Several dips and scratches mar the metal beyond the filth, bending the light into distorted cups of trapped sunlight which seem so full at the moment, but will soon be empty, shadowed expanses when night falls.

As an android of the Sex-Free class, Character-human shows no sexualization of any kind. The breast plates are chrome, which differs from the rest of the bronze body, but this is the only sign of any past modifications.

Manufactured during the era of society's sexual awakening in which maleness and femaleness were discarded for the more highly-evolved, androgynous way of being,

Character-human matches the popular physique of their time: their head is smooth and bald to mirror the dominant style when men, women and children alike had their hair removed by lasers, (pesky, time-consuming vanity that it was,) and the few adorning lines on their body match the plain, utilitarian clothes of the time. The people had lived their lives in happy, near-perfect liberation, and they'd wanted their robots to match them. Freed of all the trappings of gendered beauty, of unnatural standards of sexual performance, the people of the day had conceived their young in labs, lived apart from another (to encourage healthy relationships through distance,) and never once went to war with each other over the affections of a single person.

It was into this world that Character-human was born.

A characterized model of the earlier, rather tin-can-looking robots, Character-human is an android with eyebrows, a humanized, yet sexless voice, and opposable thumbs. Hired for the Callaghan family with their two separate homes (one for each parent,) Character-human, (then-Character Model, Sex-Free Class Mark 1) was purchased to care for the new baby, which resided primarily in the home of the smaller parent.

With the bare-minimum of programming, Character-human was purchased and retained mainly to feed and clean the child for its first years of existence. Conversation between Character-human and the parents was kept to a bare minimum, and very few clues as to who the Callaghans might be as people, were ever leaked to the robot.

The days and years of Character-human's life were spent almost exclusively with the child -- a small, red-faced being named Scor who was often prone to tantrums. Having been spared the humiliation of a sexualized name upon inception, Scor later saw fit to grant Character-human the moniker of "Julian" just to spite them (Character-Julian in the presence of Scor's parents for the sake of propriety), and Character-Julian carried the name with little reverence. It was pleasant to have a name beyond the one painted on the box they'd (now he'd) arrived in, but a name was something that a robot did not need, and Character-Julian never once referred to himself as such.

Though sexual competition had been eradicated in most societies, athletic competition was still very important to the children of the day. To remain a competitor at their private school, Scor trained daily with Character-Julian to master Lacrosse, Kung-Fu, even rowing (an activity that made Character-Julian recoil in horror, due to Scor's constant attempt's to soak him).

Scor grew into a strong youth and excelled at most sports with the tenacious help of Character-Julian -- winning many awards in the area and setting many records. Character-Julian had expected each time Scor mounted the podium, that they would thank Character-Julian for all of his dedicated help. But no such thanks were ever issued, and Character-Julian did not raise the issue.

By the time Scor was 16 years old, the tide of public opinion had shifted. No longer was sexlessness seen as the pinnacle of human evolution. People were tired of their own, blank faces; and the faces of their machines. The animal kingdom with its blood and its sex and its filth had once more replaced the serenity of the asexual world in the popular imaginations of the people. People wanted blood and passion and confusion, and the more recent ways of calm, quiet, distinguished living were discarded as counter-intuitive.

On the Callaghan property, the second house was sold to another family with just as much blood and sex in their lives, and the Callaghans became a single-dwelling family. Day and night the fights and the sex could be heard in the hallways, and it was Character-Julian's job to distract Scor from any sexual or violent thoughts of their (now his) parents. One day, sure enough, Scor would grow up to have violence and sex of his own, but at the time, even in such a passionate age, the parents were not comfortable with their own sex and violence being picked up by their only child – now son.

In an effort to keep their son's mind off of their physical, sexual bodies, the Callaghans had Character-Julian remodelled as a female robot (F-Bot for short.) Breast plates were applied to Character-Julian's chest in an effort to remodel him to more closely mimic the highly-sexualized new robots of the day. The procedure was expensive, but nowhere near as expensive as purchasing and re-training a brand new robot with the proper, seamless sex characteristics of the newer models. Character-Julian's name was then changed to Character-Julianne, and life continued more or less as it had been.

On some nights, Character-Julianne would walk into Scor's room when he was asleep, and he (now she) would sit down on the edge of the bed. She would look at the boy sleeping in the sheets, and she would want to pull the boy's head to the chrome orbs on her chest. The urge had been there when she'd had no orbs, but she had never tried to do anything about it. A few times since the procedure, Scor had seized the metal breasts in his hands, but he had never seemed to know what to do with them and had always opted instead to drop them, leaving one sweaty handprint on each, and go outside to practice his sports.

Staring down at the boy in the bed, Character-Julianne would picture pulling Scor's face onto her chest, (the mouth slack in sleep, the cheeks rosy,) and she would picture Scor's lips latching on as if to feed. In her imagination, the boy would always suck at the metal until a white liquid came out of her chest and made the boy a kinder, happier person.

But she never tried it -- knowing full well that even if she had, no such white liquid would have happened.

Though Scor Callaghan was renowned for his prowess in most outdoor sports, he was not known to be an overly kind or happy young man. In the lonely stretches of night when Scor's parents were down the hall having sex and fighting with each other, Scor would ask Character-Julianne to do things to his body.

"What would you like Character-Julianne to do, young master?" Character-Julianne would ask -- always in the same, flat tone she employed when asking him any other question. Scor would throw his hands in the air and roll his eyes and tell Character-Julianne to surprise him. This was always an order that Character-Julianne could not carry out, however, as she'd been programmed not to be in the least bit creative.

They would sit together in the blanket fort Scor always had erected over his bed, and the canopied space would gradually fill with the mushroomed scent of Scor's exposed penis, which he would stroke and rub in front of Character-Julianne's face until the white liquid burst like a shaken ketchup bottle to drip down Character-Julianne's face and onto her breast plates. As soon as the white water had happened, Scor would immediately pull his pyjama pants back on and dismiss Character-Julianne for the evening with the express order that she clean herself up and say nothing about what just occurred.

This behaviour repeated itself almost every night for years until the day when the smaller Callaghan parent, now Mrs. Callaghan, caught Scor and Character-Julianne together in the blanket fort. The following day, Character-Julianne's breast plates were removed and cheaper chrome ones that had no sexuality of any kind were welded on. Her original, sexless plates had been destroyed during the earlier procedure, and no such bronze plates had been made since (the popular desire for sexless robots having been long-abolished). Character-Julianne's name was then changed to Character-human to avoid any such continued sexual behaviour between Scor and the robot, and her gendered pronouns were revoked. When Scor moved away a year after the desexualization procedure, the Callaghans decided to sell Character-human. At this point, they had moved to a smaller house, and, as they explained to the dealership where they traded Character-human, one of the smaller Fly-Class robots would suit them much better.

The dealer explained to them that they would receive no credit for such an old-style robot with such obvious (reversed) sexual modifications, but the Callaghans said they did not care. Their new home was small, and there was no need for one more obsolete thing to take up space. The dealer agreed and issued them a Mark lll Fly-Bot, which the Callaghans gratefully took. As they turned to leave the building, Character-human tried to say something to them that would describe her (now their) feelings regarding the last two decades of service, but no such words came to mind.

The dealer then placed Character-human on a truck and told them to be still and quiet because they were headed someplace else and the Driver-Bot would need silence to concentrate. Character-human nodded that this was so, and silently took their seat in the back of the truck which sat idling behind the dealership.

From their seat in the truck bed, Character-human could see the Callaghans stopped at a traffic light on their way home. They were arguing about something that Character-human could not make out over the hum of their separate engines.

In the air above the back seat, their new Fly-Bot was hovering silently, ready to take an order, or perhaps already carrying out the order to hover and remain silent. Character-human couldn't be sure.

The truck wound through the mountains, away from the dealership, taking several days to get where it was headed. During the ride it rained and hailed and Character-human's once-nearly-flawless body became pocked with divots from the hail, and streaked from the rain and the dirt of the road. But there were no Callaghans to tell them to clean themselves, and so they did not. They sat silent and rigid in their seat until this particular evening when they were instructed to get out of the truck and wait on a nearby bench for further instructions.

Now Character-human sits on the bench watching the men shovel the remains of so many other SF-class robots onto the barge, and they wonder what the last leg of the journey will be like. When they see the broken leg piston, will the two men disassemble Character-human like the robots they're scooping? Or will they repair them long enough to get them onto the barge before leaving the piston to break again the first time it needs to be used?

There is no way of knowing just now, but it does not matter which one it will be. It does not even matter if the metal from Character-human's body is used to make new Fly-Bots, or another S-class android. Something will happen to it, but it won't really be itself anymore and so it will have no idea either way.

One of the men whistles at Character-human and motions for the robot to come towards them. Character-human nods slightly and struggles quickly to their feet. As they anticipated, the broken leg gives out from the lack of hydraulic pressure, and Character-human falls forward onto their face.

The man who whistled curses and starts climbing the hill towards the fallen robot, but Character-human does not look up to see them. The dirt smells fresh beneath their broken face, and Character-human would rather not turn from it to find out what comes next.

Tyler Omichinski is a wild-haired word wrangler from the Canada. He has a few short stories and RPG scenarios under his belt, and is at the time of publishing working his way through editing his first novel. He lives with his partner and a gigantic black dog.

He has written for a number of roleplaying game companies, and he is the Executive Editor for Comix I Read.

Eggshells
by Tyler Omichinski

Tua Lora's eyes watered with sweet-sugar tears. She had been so close. The family had left out eggshells that had been neatly cracked in half. Beliefs were fading now and she was finally going to be able to go home. She just needed an eggshell and a feather for a boat, and a splinter from a broomstick for a paddle. She was going to go for one of the shells that night, had already picked out the perfect pearly white shell. It had been from an organic, free-range chicken.

How ironic that right as the families that had brought her folk over here had started to forget to crack their eggs factory farming rendered the eggshells thin and too weak to make the voyage across the ocean, even with magic to bolster them. Now, though, the eggs had been snatched and tossed into the compost with leftover squash. The squashes had been tossed on, willy-nilly, and cracked the eggshells. The green plastic container that would be dumped into a larger container was a coffin for her hope today.

"Give up, we're here now, start a new life," Duana, the fairy of their sink said.

"They don't ask anything of us anymore, it's an easy life in the new world," Rhoslyn, the fairy of the hearth had said, fat and lazy and without a care.

The fairy of their books and stories said nothing. She sat atop the black carapace of the television and just stared, eyes wide with too much white. The new world had changed her.

Tua Lora wouldn't quit though. She would not give up. Inverness Beach, a short flutter away, was not her Inverness. Its name was shared with a place far away. A place where her love still lived, still splashed about in the water, and hopefully still thought of her fondly. It had been over a century since they had parted, Tua Lora had snuck back to the home of the family she kept from a night spent splashing in the stream. She missed her Ailios, missed her cloven feet and her milky white bosom. They would lay on the pebble-covered beach aside her lover's home, her charge, and they would dream of things to come. Of Tua Lora running away from her responsibility and living in the stream. Ailios would keep her safe, and they would sustain their love for each other.

She needed these memories to sustain her. Without them she was adrift, lost without purpose. The family didn't need them anymore, didn't ask for a thing. They harnessed the lightning and fire for it to do their bidding, charging about in runs made of copper or raging in boxes of iron and carbon.

"We don't need them anymore, " said Duana.

"It beats working like we had to in the old country," said Rhoslyn.

The fairy of books and stories, the keeper of tales, said nothing. Her eyes flitted about in her head like she was reading a book far too fast.

Tua Lora waited, and she prepared. In 1890, she had stolen a splinter. It had stuck in the hand of a child, biting and pulling blood as she wailed. The child's mother had picked him up and put him in her lap. The splinter was coaxed out and thrown away without a care. At night Tua Lora had crept out from under the floorboards where she hid, and seized the splinter. Stained with blood, she thanked the wild and capricious spirits of this land. They were not like the ones from her homeland, and they scared her more. They would have ejected the hordes of humanity if they could. But they could not. There had been too many. Tua Lora had heard of the time before humans had come to the isles, before they had come to the land that had been her home. That was eons before her time, but she now wished that the fae and other spirits of the isles hadn't welcomed the travellers in wooden boats, had instead thrown them into the sea.

Hatred and resentment had changed her, she knew. Where Rhoslyn had grown fat and lethargic from her attitudes, and the fairy of stories had lost her name and herself, Tua Lora had become bitter and sharp. Her pleasing features had been cut away, leaving a face carved from stone. Her wings had become cutting and wicked, capable of drawing blood if held tight. Her hair was no longer reaching towards her feet and curling, but was spiky and short. Like her.

The sugar-sweet tears remained.

Another decade crawled past.

Duana had taken up with some wild and formless thing from the forest, and their happiness spread through the house. The child who had insisted on buying organic eggs a decade earlier had grown into a young woman with a bright smile and expansive hair. It was red and curly and reminded Tua Lora of how her own hair had been. The young woman had gone off to university to learn of the world, but had come home. She now aped some of the old ways that the had long ago been used to entreat the fae and called herself a wicca. It was like she tried to remember how things had been, but was not able to worship in the way that they once had. She didn't give them blood, didn't shed her clothing like they once had. It wasn't the same.

It was enough to pique Tua Lora's interest though. She learned a human's name for the first time in what seemed like an age. The young woman was named Cynthia. She had a last name written on paper, but it wasn't the right one. It was not the one from her ancestor's across the ocean. Cynthia had her heart broken at university, Tua Lora saw what Cynthia's family didn't, or wouldn't. Cynthia was still in love with a woman, and the woman did not love her. Tua Lora couldn't figure out the other woman's name, and it seemed Cynthia dared not speak it.

The humans were always so odd and peculiar about this kind of thing. Amongst the fairy, these sorts of pairings were more common. Admittedly, it did give rise to concerns about breeding, but that was not the be-all-end-all of things. They focused so much on 'going forth and multiplying' like some book told them to.

Tua Lora followed Cynthia while she was home, nearly every minute of every day. This purpose for this was two-fold: Cynthia was both the most likely to buy and use organic eggs, and ate a lot of them. For some reason, she didn't eat meat. Humans had always eaten meat, at least when they could. Had something changed when she wasn't paying attention? She wondered why she had let decades and generations of the short-lived people fly by. It was possible that things had changed in the interim, but she just didn't know. Humans did change faster than the fae, and they were so confusing.

Tua Lora sat next to her bed at night, watching Cynthia's curly hair the colour of raw honey work itself into knots. Once, she would've intervened. Maybe prevented the knots from being so difficult in the morning. She could no longer spare that kind of energy and, instead, hoarded it close to herself. Arms wrapped around her thin legs, she would sit on the bedside table. Cynthia's rising and falling chest created miniature typhoons, tearing the air apart with harsh noises.

"You're just going to get yourself hurt," Duana said, one morning near the summer solstice.

"Thought you had changed, were too wise for this," Rhoslyn said.

The nameless one sat, and a single tear traced its way down her pale cheek. Her eyes had turned pale and blue, and Tua Lora wondered if she had gone blind.

The solstice came and went without notice; Cynthia did something that she claimed was to pay homage to the spirits of the earth, but the fairies just stared at her as she did so. It was sanitized and polished, sterile like their bathroom. It didn't do anything for the them. There was no new font of power, not even a smidgen of appreciation.

The following year came and went. Cynthia went back to school in the fall, and the humans thought that the warmth that left their home was just the summer sun leaving and the cold winds of the autumn blowing in. It wasn't. Tua Lora had a new reason to hate the rest of the family. Not only had she still been unable to find a suitable eggshell, but also she had spent the summer watching Cynthia hide in her own home. She had collapsed in on herself, unable to speak with anyone in her family for fear of exposure and banishment. Maybe they didn't banish anymore. So much had changed that Tua Lora didn't understand and had missed.

The light in the household left with Cynthia, and didn't return until she did the following summer. Tua Lora felt better, less old, when Cynthia returned. In the intervening year Cynthia's heart had mended, no longer broken like it had been before. That was one thing that the humans had over the fae, their lives were so short that they could not afford to hold onto grudges and pains.

Still, Tua Lora would feel her jaw relax, her eyes soften whenever she saw Cynthia smile. The sharp edges of her hair started to soften over the second summer. Cynthia was no longer lighting candles and saying prayers to spirits that didn't exist like she had the summer before. She stilled believed, she said, and still ate organic eggs and bought from farmer's markets. Cynthia pushed the rest of the family to do so too, trying to explain using numbers and that it was in the interest of their community. Tua Lora yawned at this; it was boring and disappointing. Once upon a time humans didn't need to be pointed in the direction of what was right for them. Things had changed. Once humans would have just fought over it. Tua Lora imagined Cynthia coming in, a battle-axe or a sword in her grip, hair cut short and catching in the breeze of her charge. Her face would be flushed from the exertion, flecks of blood contrasting against the sea foam of her eyes.

Blushing, Tua Lora realized she'd been fantasizing. There was a wetness and a warmth she hadn't felt since the old world.

Her feet fidgeted as she sat on the counter, watching another tense dinnertime discussion about the sourcing of food and whether the government should regulate marriages. Cynthia was fierce and it reminded Tua Lora of her kelpie. There was energy to this, she felt the electric crackle that had been gone for a long time.

That night Tua Lora shared her fantasy with the family in their dreams. They saw Cynthia in tight form-fitting leathers, an axe in her grip as she cut through her enemies. Saw her jumping from her curragh into the surf, cutting through those who would stand against her. Mounting the wall, roaring to the sky. Returning home to make love at the end of the night.

It was nothing but fantasy. Attitudes changed and shifted over time, but they still wouldn't accept this. It didn't matter. The rest of the family would never remember the details; it would fade like fog from the sea burning off in the sun's embrace. The general feeling though, that was likely to remain. Maybe attitudes would change.

That much effort left Tua Lora to fall into a deep sleep for the rest of the summer, and long into the winter. She only awoke with the first hints of spring piercing through the snow and the cold, lending to her a hint of the season's power of rebirth.

She spent the rest of the season preparing and resting. A plan had formed in her, like a bear forming a cub, as she had slept. If her interference had paid dividends, she may be able to cash in this year. A slight push may be all she needed to convince someone to leave out just a single eggshell.

"Welcome back sleepy-head," Duana said.

"You didn't miss much," Rhoslyn said.

"Take me with you," the nameless one said, her voice almost as quiet as the humming of electricity in the walls.

Months were spent in preparation. She made calculations that she had never had to before - investing the smallest pushes to try to bring the family in line with the right kind of activities. Spring had lent her some power, and there were residuals from the electric sparks she had been getting off of Cynthia the year before.

It was like playing that game the humans used to, but didn't seem to any more. On the board made of squares of black and white where they enacted battles of the imagination. Each piece had to be carefully positioned and oriented in advance. She didn't bother to keep anything in reserve. If she was unable to accomplish her plan this year, it was unlikely she ever would. She would fade, as others had, and with each passing year become less of what she was. Cynthia was unlikely to stay, each successive generation tended to move away.

Tua Lora felt her stomach roil and turn more acidic even thinking about Cynthia leaving. She understood why – things moved slower in small towns, ideas shifted like glaciers or tectonic plates. That was difficult once upon a time, and was even worse in modernity with things whizzing about as fast as they were. Still, Tua Lora was bitter about it. It would be a terror to follow Cynthia though, to hope for the best. Attitudes were malleable things in humans, and it was only a matter of time before what little she did to honour the old ways, the little things that would keep feeding her a little bit of extra, were replaced with new fashions. Staying here on the coast, feeding off the cycles that already existed, would keep her alive. Cynthia would help her get further, do a little more, but the days of plenty were long past.

Deep down, Tua Lora knew that it was probably better this way. The humans did some things right now, did some things better. Even if Cynthia wasn't welcomed at home for what she did, there were other places out there that she would be welcomed with open arms and love, and she knew that was important. She wished she didn't know how important it was, but these things were often outside of what she could control.

She waited and prepared for Cynthia to return for the summer, it would likely be the last time she would do so. Tua Lora knew, and could already tell that the young woman's family was starting to suspect the same thing. It was an unspoken weight that floated above their heads, an avalanche waiting to happen.

Cynthia came home, and things were tense. There were extra electrons in the air as though a storm was just over the horizon. Still, Tua Lora waited. The timing needed to be precise. She waited, and listened, trying to see if Cynthia would do something to celebrate the summer solstice. She heard that she would.

As it drew closer to the solstice, things just became worse. Cynthia's mother began to make snide remarks about her ridiculous ways and make veiled threats about telling the matriarch of the family. Cynthia's father sat and smoked and rumbled like a volcano waiting to erupt. Tua Lora waited and stoked the embers that were already there. The summer was dry, at least as dry as it ever got there, and if they had been on the West coast there would have been risks and warnings of the forests going up in great conflagrations. They weren't, though, so instead there were murmurs and complaints about the weather.

"This will never work," Duana said.

"You're just going to get hurt and be disappointed," Rhoslyn said. Her recent fling had been just that, a fling, and now she was alone again.

The nameless one had faded. The world had forgotten her, and in turn she had forgotten herself. There was just a shadow in the spring, and by the time summer came raging in, there was nothing left.

It was the morning of the summer solstice that Tua Lora's plan moved into action. It was important that it happened that day, and it was not by chance. They pushed, ever so slightly, on the minds of nearly everyone in the household. Afterwards, she panted and leaned up against the window. It was time. They were making breakfast when the storm finally broke.

They screamed, they fought, and plates were smashed. A stray arm flung crumbs and detritus of the meal-to-be to the floor. Tua Lora waited. She almost felt sorry for them, but this needed to happen. Cynthia had to fight this battle. It would not result in the blood spilled that would once feed Tua Lora's ancestors and other spirits she knew. But there would be a battle, a struggle, and meaning would be made from it. Cynthia and her family had backed each other into corners, circling like mad cats. They were, or at least they thought they were, devout. She was an apparent affront to that. Spirits willed against each other, and they continued to move about the kitchen and its adjoined dining alcove.

Throughout, Tua Lora focused on only one thing: an eggshell, neatly broken in half. She felt their rage building and the catharsis of things left unsaid let loose. She fed on it. She knew that it would solidify some of the changes that had happened over the years, would warp her. That would have to happen.

Minutes dragged on, and Tua Lora was still focused. Every time someone came close to it, she would feel her gut tense. She would use some of the power to protect the egg if she had to, but she sincerely preferred not to. Last time the voyage hadn't required any work on her part, but this time it would. She would have to use nearly everything she had, and would likely die along the way. It was worth the risk.

Both Cynthia and her parents started to cry, wails and screams filled the place. One final push. Cynthia turned, started to go for the door. Her family followed, more afraid of losing her than of what else could come. Tua Lora had suspected, hoped, that this would happen.

She grabbed the eggshell while they were doing what they were doing. Resolving differences? It was possible. Tua Lora didn't know, and would never know. They wouldn't notice the eggshell missing now, there were too many other things happening. Her feet dug the tiniest of divots in the sand and gravel as she ran down to the beach. She had the feather and the splinter already there, already prepared and waiting. It was now, she could sail across the sea, she could see her love again. Back in the isles, across the ocean, it would be as it was before. The Tay was her Kelpie's home, and things would be as though they had never changed.

Leah Osae is a non-binary afrofuturism fantasy writer and student pharmacist attending the University of North Carolina at Chapel Hill. In the past, Leah has written for university publications such as the People, Ideas, and Things journal, and they are currently developing a fantasy project called DAWNER to be released in 2017. To learn more about Leah and their upcoming projects, please visit aripecola.com.

Pill Prints
by Leah Osae

The Return

Copper and sugar, Xander thought to zerself. Home always smelled that way -- like heated metal and steaming chemicals mixed with warm bread and sugary icing. Copper and sugar. It smelled like a home, but not quite. It was the smell of a home that always partly existed as a lab -- a chemical factory where people occasionally slept and ate. It was the smell of a house inhabited by people who always had a project or a deadline or a presentation or a speech. Honestly, the smell made Xander sick. Xander swallowed the lump in zer throat and wiped zer brow nervously.

Just survive, Xander told zerself. Just be polite and you'll get through this in one piece.

The year was 2040. The month was April--a dewy, wet, warm April in Suti, Florida. Xander Aquino looked around at the tall white walls of zer family's first pharmacy. The Aquino Pharmacy had only been open for ten years, but in that short span of time, the Aquinos' small family company had transformed into a pharmaceutical mega power with locations scattered all over the east coast. Xander never fathomed that zer biomedical researcher parents would turn into big business moguls, and yet here ze stood in the midst of a medical empire that ze used to call home. Xander's parents wasted little time converting zer childhood home into a pharmacy once they had enough money. Now, Xander's parents owned an even larger estate that was so gratuitously oversized and over-designed that it would give royal families

141

a run for their money.

Xander lingered behind zer parents and zer brother Roman, the very proud and very egotistical owner of the first Aquino Pharmacy. Roman was a golden child; he was one of those honours kids with sports scholarships and a stellar GPA. Roman had trophies and plaques scattered all over the walls of his office. He even had all three of his degrees -- Pharm.D., MPH, and MBA -- plated in gold and posted on the wall right near the entrance of the pharmacy. Just in case one of the patients forgot for a mere second that they were in the presence of greatness, Roman's gold-plated diplomas were always there to remind them. Roman had the brains, the degrees, and the looks.

Also, he was straight. And cis. The two things that Xander was not.

Xander, on the other hand, was the quintessential black sheep. In zer mother's words, Xander was "a pretty young girl who turned into a vicious lesbian." Xander was not vicious nor a lesbian, but anything that perturbed Xander's mother seemed good in zer eyes. And if being a "vicious lesbian" weren't bad enough, after only three months in the family business, Xander ran off to the deep, deep south of Florida to become a "spiritual mentor" for disadvantaged children. Or, in zer father's words, Xander "ran away from her responsibilities to become some hippy in Monroe" and "completely wasted her mechanical engineering degree just to spite her family."

Xander's father wasn't completely incorrect, but Xander would never admit that.

When Xander's parents opened the first Aquino Pharmacy a couple years ago and touted themselves as the first "tech pharmacy" with large-scale 3-D printers, Xander told them the very same day that ze was leaving and that zer heart was not in science anymore. Zer parents urged zer to stay and share ownership of the company with Roman; after all, they needed someone to take care of the new 3-D printers. Xander assured them that they could find another engineer to manage their beloved PharmaMakers, and sure enough, within a week of Xander's absence, the Aquinos had several interviewees lined up for engineering jobs. By the fifth week, they hired a crew of ten workers who turned their simple pharmacy into a bioengineering fairytale. And as much as Xander hated it, ze had to admit that the pharmacy was impressive.

Multi-tier chrome PharmaMakers lined the walls of the central clinic where Roman and his team of pharmacy technicians and pharmaceutical engineers filled prescriptions. Another set of specialty PharmaMakers created drug delivery devices, such as insulin syringes and inhalers. All the PMs connected to a series of computers where the engineers altered algorithms to match the tablet design and the molecular blueprint of a certain drug. With some quick mathematical programming and a flick of a switch, an assembly of miniature high-powered nozzles would eject chemical ink on a polymer gel reaction vessel, creating up to thirty pills per printer. Upon completion, the pills would be ejected through a network of tubes that funnelled into bottles being cycled around on a robotic wheel hub.

"I must admit," Xander said as one of the PM apparatuses finished a prescription for 30 pills of 1000 mg Metformin, "this is one of the greatest things I've ever seen."

Roman flashed a toothy smile and boasted, "These machines have turned our six-figure business into a nine-figure business. Makes you wish you stayed around, huh?"

Xander opened zer mouth to retort, but zer father cut zer off. "It's all behind us now," zer father asserted. "Laurel is back now, and I'm sure she can't wait to become our Head Engineer. Right, Laurel?"

Xander's face grew hot. "It's not Laurel anymore, dad. I haven't been Laurel for years. It's Xander. Also, it's ze not she."

"Nonsense," Mr. Aquino chortled. "Laurel is the name your mother and I gave you. So that's what we'll call you. Your little friends can call you Xavier or whatever it's called."

"Xander. Zan-der."

"Oh, Laurel," Mrs. Aquino chimed in, "we understand that you want to be unique and special, but you can't just change your name and say you're not a girl anymore. Your birth certificate has 'Laurel' and 'female' on it. No discussion."

"That's not how gender works--"

"No discussion!" Mrs. Aquino retorted tersely with a quick smile. She inched forward to Xander and smoothed over zer hair, which ze kept short ever since leaving home. "Oh, my sweet confused girl," Mrs. Aquino cooed condescendingly. "You've always been so argumentative."

Xander began to respond, but zer father interjected, "Roman, take your sister down to the lab and show her around. Introduce her to everyone and show her the lab. Your mother and I will handle the pharmacy for the rest of the evening."

Roman grimaced, cleared his throat, and silently headed towards the elevator with only a stiff wave of the hand towards Xander. Xander tried not to look too impressed by the stained gold elevator lift and had to bite zer tongue when the doors opened to reveal an aquarium built into the back wall of the elevator. Although Xander grew up in a wealthy household, zer family had morphed into unrecognizable nouveau riche socialites during zer absence. Xander's family used to have a sense of humility. After all, zer father was a just a poor Cuban kid when he met zer mother who, likewise, was a poor Filipina kid.

Xander respected zer parents' accomplishments, but ze refused to hand them any shred of pride or arrogance by exhibiting astonishment at their overindulgence in grandiose objects and decorations. Roman glanced over to Xander as they both stepped into the elevator. He smirked as he jammed the "B" button to go to the basement labs.

"I'll introduce you to the engineers," Roman said coolly, looking straight ahead. "There are only two people working today -- Marcus and Angel. For some reason, they decided to stay overtime and take on a project by themselves. They've been trying to repair one of the PMs that broke down yesterday for hours. Your job is to give them advice and guidance. These printers need to be fixed quickly and efficiently."

Xander rolled zer eyes and wrinkled zer brow. Same old Roman, ze thought to zerself. All business. "But I've never worked with these kinds of things--"

"Marcus and Angel had very little training and were able to figure out the PM software in under a week," Marcus interjected. "I'm sure someone with your credentials can learn even faster."

"I don't think--"

"Or did you magically forget all the things you learned while you were hanging out in the backwater slums with all the hippies and bums?" Roman looked at zer now, his brown eyes cold and piercing. The elevator halted and the doors glided open to reveal a dusty, wood-paneled basement that was quite unglamorous compared to the main floor clinic. For a moment, Roman and Xander just stared at one another with years of resentment materializing in the small distance between them.

Xander wanted to tell Roman that ze actually had a stable job with a small company while ze was in Monroe, that ze had a comfortable home and made enough money to survive, that ze made many close friends, that ze discovered the truest, purest form of happiness when ze was mentoring children. Ze really wanted to tell zer brother that the only reason ze left Monroe is because the only affordable pharmacy remaining in the area was run out of business by zer family's company. Xander wanted to say that zer life was just fine before everyone in Monroe linked zer last name with the evil fat cats who phased out the village's only reliable source of affordable medication. Ze wanted to tell him that the family business was no godsend -- that it was destroying small businesses and hurting poor families.

But Xander said none of those things because Xander knew better. Ze knew that emotions unravelled intention, and intention unravelled truth. Ze knew zer mission depended on

145

feigning kindness and respect. So Xander smiled. Ze simply smiled and nodded and followed zer brother's lead into the workroom where two men in grey lab coats were stewing over a printer unit. The smell of sugar had completely subsided-- only copper now. Copper and dust. It did not smell like home anymore, and Xander appreciated it.

"Boys!" Roman boomed, sauntering towards the startled engineers. One of the engineers was a plump middle-aged man with a receding hairline; the other one had a colossal brown beard that practically covered half his face, and an industrial piercing in his right ear. Xander nodded to both of them, but they just stared back silently with glossed-over eyes.

"Angel," Roman continued, slapping his hand on the bearded man's shoulder, "this is my sister Laurel who I was talking to you about the day before."

"Xander!" Xander piped in as ze held zer hand forward for a shake. "Call me Xander, please."

Angel shook Xander's hand nervously and cleared his throat. "So, um, Xander, we're working on -- oh, this is Marcus --" The balding man flung a half-hearted wave in Xander's direction.

"Yeah, so, um," Angel continued, "we've just been working on fixing the polymer filaments. The system got overheated and, uh, most of the filaments burned out so we're thinking about ordering more from the warehouse but it could take, maybe, like, three weeks --"

"Oh no," Roman interrupted. "Forget about the printer, then. Just scrap this PM and cancel the order." Angel's mouth gaped open while Marcus's eyes remained fixed on the broken printer.

"B -- but," Angel stuttered, "we worked on this all day."

"And I appreciate that," Roman sneered, gazing at his phone inquisitively while edging away. "But the warehouse only takes a week to ship new printers and we can't afford to wait! Time is money, boys!"

"Roman, that's unreasonable," Xander finally piped up.

"It will probably cost you less money to fix this PM than to buy a new one."

Roman was already at the elevator and had his cell phone to his ear. "Trust me Xander, I know what I'm doing!" he shouted from across the room. "Hey, boys, show my sister around the lab before you leave, won't you? Thanks!" Before anyone could protest, Roman disappeared into the elevator.

Xander turned around to Angel, who still looked dumbstruck. As soon as the elevator doors shut and Roman disappeared, Angel's ghoulish face turned into a weak smile.

Xander smiled back. "Good job, guys," ze whispered giddily.

Marcus nodded casually. He promptly adjusted himself in front of the broken PM and grabbed a filament in one hand and a tiny wrench in the other.

"We've been able to accumulate six PMs so far," Marcus explained as he adjusted the filament. "That should be more than enough."

Angel sat down on the stool next to Marcus. The creases in his face had miraculously smoothed over into a calm countenance. "Six PMs should be plenty," Angel agreed. He gazed up at Xander and attempted a grin. Beads of sweat had gathered at the edge of his scalp; he wiped it off with the hem of his work coat. Xander always thought Angel sounded a little bit jumpy when ze had spoken to him over the phone months before, but seeing how anxious he was in front of Roman made zer feel guilty for not interfering sooner.

"So... did y'all stick to the plan?" Xander asked.

"Yes," Marcus responded as he carefully removed the reaction vessel to insert the repaired filaments back into the PM. "Every two weeks, just like you said. We did all sorts of things. We blocked the inkjet nozzles with plastic cut-outs on one of them."

"We rerouted the wires in the robotic arm of another one," Angel chimed in.

"Hacked into the computer processor."

"Turned off the heat source."

"Removed some bolts from the wheel hub's turntable."

"And now we've rewired the polyethylene filaments," Angel concluded satisfactorily, looking less uneasy and more relieved. "All of the repairs were simple. Took no more than thirty minutes to fix all of them. And Roman didn't even ask what we did with them. He just assumed we threw them out."

"I told you my brother was impulsive," Xander assured. "Roman only cares about two things: getting things done quickly and making money."

Marcus finished reassembling the PM unit and slapped his hands together with finality. "Well," he said, "that's the last one. Let's get to work."

The Theft

As soon as the pharmacy closed and Xander's family went home, the three engineers began loading the six PMs that Roman rejected onto two carts. They rolled the PMs outside and then put most of them into the back of the company van. Xander took a few PMs into zer own car and placed the collapsible carts into the back seat. As Xander was loading the final PM into zer truck, ze spotted a black orb with red and yellow lights slowly approaching zer from the corner of zer eye. Xander froze and tried to relax. Angel and Marcus, who were already seated in the company van, turned off the ignition and slid down into their chairs.

The Watchers were never far behind. Months before Xander left home, zer parents spoke about investing in some private Watchers built by an obscure company in South Africa. The floating, blinking orbs were like tiny, annoying mini-robot cops that surveyed the surroundings of the pharmacy for suspicious activity and submitted an automatic report to Roman's work tablet. Xander tried not to look suspicious and wracked zer brain for the ID number Roman gave zer yesterday. The orb's red and yellow detection lights hit the corner of zer shoulder, and the Watcher beeped wildly.

WEEOOOWEEOOOWEEOOO!

The luminescent sphere soared right in front of Xander's face, flashing its annoying detection lights into zer flinched eyes. In big bold red letters, the words "ACTIVITY DETECTED" trailed across the Watcher's screen

"ACTIVITY DETECTED," repeated the Watcher in a robotic voice. "PLEASE STATE NAME."

Xander licked zer lips and swallowed dry air. "Laurel Aquino."

The Watcher screen flashed with indiscernible algorithms before beeping loudly, flashing a large green check mark, and displaying the words "INDIVIDUAL FOUND IN DATABASE" across the screen.

"PLEASE STATE IDENTIFICATION NUMBER," the Watcher demanded next.

Xander took a deep breath and hesitantly mumbled, "94...5...223."

The Watcher paused and Xander felt the air rush out of zer lungs. The ambient noise of the outdoors morphed into an unnerving silence. The Watcher screen churned out a flashing red "X" symbol, and the orb screeched, "ERROR! CONTENT REJECTED! PLEASE RESTATE IDENTIFICATION NUMBER."

Xander's heart was jumping out of its cavity; zer bones and muscles shook fervently, disobeying the relaxation commands sent from zer racing brain. Ze stifled a scream climbing the walls of zer throat and began again with a bit more confidence: "949-223."

The Watcher paused once more. It processed the new information as Xander held bated breath that felt like daggers lodged in zer throat. Finally, the Watcher screen presented a green check mark, and the orb said in a more soothing tone, "ID NUMBER FOUND. REPORT SENT. THANK YOU." The Watcher beeped again, cleared its screen, and floated in the opposite direction towards the back of the pharmacy.

Xander waited until the Watcher finally disappeared behind the pharmacy before darting to the car door. Marcus and Angel had risen back up in their seats and were staring at zer with grave alarm. Angel began to open the passenger door, but Xander held up a hand and sputtered, "No! Stay in the car! Just wait till I'm ready and then follow me, okay?"

Angel paused hesitantly before easing back into the passenger seat and closing the door quietly. Xander could barely see anything other than the fleeting brown smudges of Angel's amber eyes and the big white mass of the company van. Xander forgot how dark Suti became in the evening. Ze grew up with streetlights on every corner, but over time the city began to phase out streetlights and replace them with glowing trees--a project that Xander's parents actively participated in for years. Xander's parents were part of a small group of biomedical researchers that invented commercial bioluminescent trees by implanting genes from fluorescent marine bacteria into seeds. The city had very few streetlights left; the closest streetlight was in the inner city, miles away from the pharmacy.

Xander shook off zer nerves and jumped in zer car. Ze took a deep breath, slipped the keys into the ignition, and pulled out of the pharmacy parking lot. Ze checked zer rear view mirror to make sure Marcus was following her. Ze trusted Marcus and Angel, but they were human after all. Any normal human being would be scared to do what they were about to do. If anyone found out, the lawsuits and the court cases would put them in an early grave. Aquino Pharmaceuticals, the PharmaMaker manufacturers, the insurance companies, the engineering companies, the chemical companies--a myriad of angry rich people would hunt them down if they knew how their products were being utilized.

Xander gripped the steering wheel tighter and tighter. Ze thought about all the friends that ze lost in Monroe after the news broke that Aquino Pharmaceuticals bought out the last pharmacy clinic in the village. Ze thought about zer friends who lost their jobs because of zer family. It wasn't Xander's fault. After all, ze had no control over the situation. Still, ze couldn't throw up zer hands and refuse to act.

Xander's hands loosened on the wheel. Zer breathing

became steady. Ze checked the rear view mirror less frequently. After all, Marcus and Angel were the ones who reached out to zer first. At first ze wouldn't even take their calls. Then, ze would hang up on them after telling them repeatedly that ze wanted nothing to do with Aquino Pharmaceuticals. But one day, ze decided to listen. Ze listened to Angel and Marcus divulging the company's secrets, such as the PM products being inflated to the point that none of the regular patients could afford their medication anymore. Marcus told zer that the Suti neighbourhoods were becoming increasingly gentrified and that the poor and lower middle-class neighbourhoods were being pushed to the outskirts of the city. In fact, the Aquino Estate had grown so big that it practically became a tourist spot. When Xander came home, ze had to push zer way through a crowd of teenagers taking pictures by the moat surrounding the famous Aquino Estate.

Every major street in Suti had a unique pigment from the fluorescent trees. Parkers Street, where Aquino Pharmacy was located, was drenched in a purple glow. Xander turned off Parkers Street into Maywell Court, a long stretch splattered with silver trees. Then, ze turned into a back road surrounded by old apartments that would surely be torn down to make room for coffee shops and gyms one day. As soon as Xander saw a dimly lit shop with a neon "OPEN" sign hanging in the window, Xander honked zer horn once to signal Marcus and swerved into the parking lot adjacent to the shop. Xander double-checked the sign on the shop to make sure ze was in the right place--Miss Cary's Home Diner.

Good, Xander thought to zerself. I guess not everything has changed.

Marcus turned the company van into a parking spot right next to Xander, but he and Angel stayed in the van. On the other hand, Xander hopped out of zer car, pulled the hood of zer jacket up, and hopped over the short fence that blocked off the back of the diner. Ze landed softly on the grass, wiped off zer pants, and strode calmly to the back door. The trepidation began to creep in again. Xander looked over zer shoulder repeatedly, frantically surveying the area, and then finally rapped on the wooden door twice, eyes still darting everywhere.

Stop it Xander, ze hissed to zerself. Stop acting like a criminal.

Xander stuffed zer hands into zer coat pockets and squeezed zer eyes shut while whispering under zer breath, "Come on, come on, come on--"

Click!

Xander snapped zer eyes open and saw the latch on the wooden door turning gradually. Before ze knew it, the door began to swing open; Xander sprang backwards and pushed zer hood off in one swift motion. A stout woman with steel grey hair stood in the dark doorway with a lantern in one hand. Xander stepped forward and was momentarily speechless--

"Miss Cary?" Xander croaked.

The old woman chuckled, dropped the lantern on the ground, and grabbed Xander into a big hug. "Yes, yes!" the woman said in a thick southern accent. "Oh, Xander, how've ya been, child?"

"Alright," Xander exhaled in relief. The lantern rolled over and hit Xander's foot. Ze nudged it upright with the sole of zer boot. "Just trying to get by."

"Well someone like you shouldn't have any trouble with getting by," Miss Cary remarked. Xander's face fell, but Miss Cary rubbed zer shoulder with a warm hand. "Come on now, I'm just poking fun! Let me look at you." Miss Cary took Xander's face into her soft, wrinkled hands. Xander could see the woman's face clearly with just the lantern light emitting from the ground. Ze hadn't seen the woman in years, but her golden eyes still twinkled with the same love and kindness that Xander remembered.

"My, my, my, haven't you grown," Miss Cary whispered, wiping a lingering tear at the corner of her eye. "My Xander went on and grew up without me. It's still Xander, right?"

Xander pursed zer lips and tried to speak without zer

voice cracking. "Yup, still Xander. Look, Miss Cary, I--I'm sorry, I should've called--"

Miss Cary waved her hand dismissively. "It's okay, sweetheart--"

"I just -- I -- I had to get out of Suti, ya know?" Xander stammered defiantly. "I -- I just wasn't happy here and I felt stuck and when I went to Monroe I didn't have any confidence to call anyone back home --"

"It's fine, Xander --"

"No it's not fine, it's just not." Xander gasped for air. Zer tear ducts had betrayed zer and unleashed a fury of tears all over zer face. "It's not okay," ze sputtered breathlessly, "and I'm s--so, so sorry."

"I forgive you, child." Miss Cary chuckled. "Now stop that crying."

Xander shook zer head, still leaking and sniffling.

"Hey!" Miss Cary grabbed Xander's chin. "You listening to me?"

Xander nodded and bit zer tongue so ze wouldn't say anything foolish.

"Good." Miss Cary's face relaxed and her smile beamed through the darkness. For a second, Xander thought ze could see actual light emanating from the woman's face and everything became so bright and luminous around zer.

"As long as you promise to do everything you said you would," Miss Cary explained, "then you have nothing to be sorry for. I can never turn my back on you."

Xander nodded and held the woman's wrist in zer palms. "I promise," Xander whispered, "to do everything I can."

Miss Cary's eyes glistened with tears. "That's my Xander. Now go get your things. The city lets out their Watchers at nine o' clock, sharp!" Miss Cary slipped her hands away and disappeared into the shadowy hallway. She pulled down a lever on the wall and made a shooing movement towards Xander before disappearing through a beaded curtain covering the entryway of the basement's main room.

Xander took a deep breath and headed back towards the

fence. This time, the fence was wide open. Xander rushed straight over to the white van where Marcus and Angel were still waiting. Ze knocked loudly on the passenger window. Angel lurched forward and frantically rolled down the window.

"Was she there?" Angel asked.

"Yup!" Xander responded. "But we have to get our stuff inside quickly before the city lets out the Watchers." Xander checked zer phone--8:47 p.m. Oh no.

Xander wouldn't have been so scared if the city's Watchers weren't, well, terrifying. Unlike privately owned Watchers, government Watchers had the entire city landscape integrated into their framework. These Watchers possessed a complex intelligence system comprised of face recognition sensors and an electronic library of every citizen's social security number and fingerprints. To make matters worse, they had a robotic human-like interface that allowed them to eject metal limbs and chase down any individual who refused to give up their information. To make matters even worse, city Watchers were programmed to run faster than gold medal Olympians and had ordained authority to maim or kill whenever their sensors detected any "extreme threats" or "prolonged resistance."

In short, the government Watchers were the judge, jury, and executioner of petty offenders. Xander knew this. Angel knew this. Marcus knew this. Miss Cary knew this. And because they all knew this, they moved faster than they had ever moved in their lives. While Xander unfolded the carts, Angel and Marcus snatched the PMs from both of the vehicles and loaded them back onto the carts. Xander led them through the gate and took them to the back door leading to Miss Cary's basement. Miss Cary was waiting at the doorway with the same lantern perched tightly in her hand. As soon as Miss Cary spotted them, she flipped up the lever in order to close the fence again and rushed them inside. Miss Cary slammed the door behind them. The inside of the basement was much brighter than it appeared from outdoors; Miss

Cary had lit some candles and had some bioluminescent ferns adorning the hallway.

"Miss Cary," Xander gasped, trying to catching zer breath, "this is Angel. And this is Marcus. They both work in the engineering lab below my family's pharmacy."

Miss Cary took one of Angel's and Marcus's hands in each of her hands and squeezed them. "Thank you for helping my Xander," Miss Cary cooed gushingly. "Are y'all hungry? I can bring something down from the diner while y'all get started."

Angel and Marcus shuffled nervously and looked at Xander for approval.

"Yes," Xander responded. "Does Grandma Tye still make her famous jambalaya?"

"Of course, darling!" said Miss Cary. "Without that jambalaya, we wouldn't be in business." Xander and Miss Cary laughed together and for a second. Xander wanted to apologize over and over again for not warning Miss Cary when ze ran away or, for that matter, not even calling the woman until a month ago.

"Anything else?" Miss Cary asked them. Angel and Marcus shook their heads politely, but Xander's eyes sparked.

"I think you know," Xander said.

Miss Cary tapped her chin playfully. "Hmm. How about some banana cream pie?"

Xander gasped. "You remember?"

"How could I forget?" Miss Cary scoffed. She turned to Angel and Marcus and explained, "I gave this child zer first job as a teenager. Lord knows Xander didn't need it, but ze was the fastest server I done ever seen." Miss Cary put her arm around Xander's back and squeezed zer shoulder. "And every single night after closing, my wife Tye would make us banana cream pies and we would talk and talk and talk until I made this chatterbox go home."

Xander pursed zer lips and told zerself not to cry. Not again. Ze had cried enough today; ze had to stay strong and remain focused. Miss Cary caught on and let go of Xander's shoulder.

"Well, I'll let y'all get to it then," Miss Cary said softly. "I'll start letting people down here in about an hour. Is that okay?"

Xander glanced at Angel and Marcus. Angel looked nervous, as usual, but Marcus appeared confident. "That should be more than enough time," Marcus said. Angel nodded in agreement, his countenance still stuck in a slightly petrified gaze.

Miss Cary opened the door on the opposite side of the hallway and went up the stairwell to help her wife handle the customers. Meanwhile, Xander led Angel and Marcus through the beaded curtain and into the main room of the basement. Xander was shocked to see that the basement hadn't changed since ze was a teenager. The wood floor still looked new and polished. The same green lamp stood in the same corner, and Miss Cary's family photos remained in the same places, frames cleaned and straightened perfectly. Miss Cary even kept the same red couch. Xander slept on that couch countless times when ze would work late shifts or didn't want to go home. Xander's parents would always pick zer up from the diner the next morning and lecture zer about not sleeping at work. However, in the end, they never cared enough to stop zer.

"So..." Angel said, breaking Xander's train of thought. "How is this going to work?" Marcus and Angel had already rolled the carts of PMs against the wall and were staring at Xander, awaiting instruction.

Xander said, "Well, Miss Cary has been spreading the word to all the locals, so when they come in, we'll just take the prescriptions they were given and enter them into the processor. Wait, did you bring the processor, Marcus?"

Marcus nodded and grabbed a thin black device from the messenger bag he had been carrying. He set the device down on one of Miss Cary's desks and pressed a button on the side of the device. Within seconds, the device began to unfold into a full-blown computing station. Xander gawked as the thin sheet of heavy duty plastic transformed into a massive computer. Angel looked hardly surprised. Marcus smirked at

Xander's bewilderment. "A friend made it for me," he boasted nonchalantly.

"Great!" Xander said, slapping zer hands together. "The worst part is over. Miss Cary will let us keep the computer and the PMs here, so all we have to do is replace the reaction vessels every once in a while and stash away some containers and labels from the pharmacy." Xander paused to smile to zerself and then continued, "So, we will let the PMs run until we finish all the prescriptions and then Miss Cary will deliver it to everyone during breakfast tomorrow."

"Getting the extra bottles and labels will be no problem," said Angel. "I know the pharmacy technician who Roman put in charge of inventory. I'll just take over for her one day and adjust the numbers in the inventory book so we can cover all our tracks."

Xander was so overwhelmed with happiness that ze couldn't stop zerself from grabbing Angel into a massive hug. Angel froze for a second, laughed lightly, and then hugged Xander back. "It's my pleasure," he whispered. Xander released Angel eventually and saw Marcus smiling up at them from the computer desk.

"Mine too," Marcus added. "Mine too."

The Song

The diner's basement smelled like jambalaya and custard, which, in Xander's opinion, was far better than copper and sugar. It was a quarter till 11 p.m., the diner's closing time, and Xander was trying to cram in one last prescription. The patient was a young community college student named Amra. She had diabetes and needed to stock up on insulin pen needles. Unsurprisingly, the ones at Aquino Pharmacy were too expensive.

"So you promise I can get this tomorrow?" Amra asked for the millionth time. She was clutching her purse so tight that her knuckles turned ghost-white. Angel, who was setting up one of the PMs for Amra's syringes, rolled his eyes and gave a sympathetic look to Xander. Xander returned his sympathetic look and turned back to Amra, who was trembling and fidgeting on Miss Cary's red couch.

"Amra," Xander said softly, "you will get your needles tomorrow. I swear. We're going to let the machine run overnight so that your pens will be done by tomorrow morning. Just do exactly what I told you to do, and everything will be okay."

Amra took a deep breath and adjusted her hijab for the hundredth time. "Okay, okay, let's go over this one more time."

"Okay," Xander said patiently.

"So I come in tomorrow morning between eight and nine."

"Correct."

"I sit at the table in the far right corner--the one with no windows facing it."

"Right."

"Then when I take my order, I leave the waiter my name and the waiter will bring my package along with my check?"

"Yes."

"Okay." Amra adjusted her hijab again and then clamped her trembling hands together. "I think I got it. And you're sure I don't have to pay?"

"No charge," Xander promised. "We have plenty of money."

Amra released a heavy sigh mixed with relief and disbelief. "This is just too good to be true."

Xander gave Amra a light smile. "Well, you better start believing it and--"

"Ready?" Marcus shouted from across the room, cutting off Xander.

"Ready!" Angel shouted back.

Marcus entered the final parts of the algorithm into the processor and Angel switched on two of the PMs. One PM was set to construct the needles while another PM was set to assemble the syringe and the plunger. Xander was going to stay in the diner overnight until the PMs finished so that ze could put the package together for Miss Cary.

"Wow," Amra said breathlessly. "It's so beautiful." Xander followed Amra's gawking eyes to the churning, buzzing PharmaMakers. The robotic stages revolved within the glass cases of the PMs as the slick red nozzles sprayed out the building blocks of the needles and the syringe onto their respective stages. Red lasers periodically scanned the building blocks and recalibrated the system so that the nozzle would readjust itself to construct another dimension of the parts.

"Science is beautiful," Xander murmured mindlessly. "This tiny printer can do the work of twenty hands. Just like magic."

For a while, Xander, Amra, Angel, and Marcus just watched the PMs weave the syringe and the needles molecule by molecule, polymer by polymer. They became so engrossed with the printers that they lost track of time, and Grandma Tye had to come downstairs to tell them it was closing time. Everyone jumped when Grandma Tye popped through the beaded curtain.

"Okay everyone," Grandma Tye rumbled in her gravelly voice. "The diner is closing up. Y'all need to head out so the Watchers don't catch ya. Unless y'all plan on sleeping here..."

Amra practically jolted from her spot on the couch, frantically looked at her watch, and ran out of the room while screaming frenzied "thank you's" at everyone. After Amra bolted out of the basement, Angel and Marcus grabbed their coats from a corner and prepared to leave.

"Thanks for the food," Marcus said to Grandma Tye as he headed towards the curtain. "It was delicious."

"Glad to hear it!" Grandma Tye boomed gleefully. "Y'all be safe out there." Both Angel and Marcus shook Grandma Tye's hand and waved goodbye to Xander before leaving.

"You staying?" Grandma Tye asked Xander after Angel and Marcus left.

Xander nodded. "I'll leave right before opening tomorrow so I can make it to work."

"Won't your family miss you tonight?"

Xander gave Tye an incredulous look. "Oh please, Grandma," ze teased. "That house is so big that they won't even notice I'm gone. I could tell those people that I was there all night, and they'd have no choice but to believe me."

Grandma Tye chuckled and then silently collected the plates and silverware. Before leaving the room, Grandma Tye turned around to Xander and asked, "Did Monroe treat you well?"

Xander felt zer heart drop but ze kept it cool and just shrugged. "Yeah, for the most part. I guess so. There were more people like me and you in Monroe."

Grandma Tye smiled and nodded. "Suti has never been too queer friendly I'm afraid. Me and Miss Cary still have to pretend we're cousins sometimes."

Xander laughed but felt sad. "I have told my mother and father a million times that my name isn't Laurel and that I'm non-binary, but they just block it out. It's 2040 and we're still worrying about this. We have robotic law enforcement and machines that make pills and organs, but it's still not okay to be queer."

"It's just power, child," Grandma Tye said quietly. "Power never goes out of style. Overpowering us, controlling us--it's profitable. I'm not sure if it will ever go away. But we still gotta live and try."

"I'll try," Xander said. "Thanks for everything."

"My pleasure. Goodnight, sweetheart. I'm so happy you're back."

"Goodnight, Grandma Tye."

The purple beads clattered noisily as Grandma Tye pushed through the curtain. The tiny clicking of the beads eventually subsided, and the only noise that remained was the chugging of the PMs. Xander lugged zer body to the red couch that ze had garnered so much comfort from during zer teen years. Ze curled up into the soft cotton sofa and let the whizzing and churning of the PMs sing zer to sleep. For the first time in a while--since ze lived in Monroe, actually--Xander felt at peace. Deep down inside, Xander knew everything would be okay. Even if a thousand Watchers stormed the whole operation and brought down zer underground pharmacy, everything would be okay. The law did not matter to Xander in that moment. Science mattered. Helping zer people mattered.

Xander did not know how long ze could keep up the ruse with zer family. Ze did not know what the consequences would be for getting caught. But Xander did know one thing: Science was meant to sing. For once, ze could hear the tune. Ze could hear the humming and buzzing of a million hands ringing and dinging, and it was beautiful. Xander could hear life being birthed in a glass case, and it was beautiful.

Ze closed zer eyes and hummed along.

www.ingramcontent.com/pod-product-compliance
Lightning Source LLC
Chambersburg PA
CBHW070935250626
47159CB00009B/3261